THE LAST FLAGSHIP

THE SCIENCE OFFICER: VOLUME 6

BLAZE WARD

KNOTTED ROAD PRESS

The Last Flagship
Volume 6
Blaze Ward
Copyright © 2017 Blaze Ward
All rights reserved
Published by Knotted Road Press
www.KnottedRoadPress.com

ISBN: 978-1-943663-59-0

Cover art:
Copyright © Luca Oleastri - Dreamstime.com | Cargo Spaceship in Asteroid Field

Cover and interior design copyright © 2017 Knotted Road Press

Never miss a release!
If you'd like to be notified of new releases, sign up for my newsletter.

I only send out newsletters once a quarter, will never spam you, or use your email for nefarious purposes. You can also unsubscribe at any time.

http://www.blazeward.com/newsletter/

BOOK SEVENTEEN: AVALON

JAVIER HAD the door to his workshop locked. Partly for safety reasons. Mostly just to keep people from wandering aimlessly in and wanting to *chat*. Even on a starship in flight, that happened.

His manners were generally up to chatting. Just not today.

He could be alone here. Just him and his junk. And Suvi.

His AI sidekick sat in her little armed probe, watching. It was like a giant, gray eyeball, bigger than his head, smaller than his shoulders, parked on her charging ring with a slobbering amount of music, books, and videos stored down in the base, in case she got bored.

The rest of the room was an organized mess.

He had redone everything when he'd first claimed the space. Turned the shelves into clear-faced drawers so he could see what was in them, while still keeping it all from flying around if they lost power to the gravplates, which happened less frequently than it used it. Stuck things into drawers with a filing system that existed only in his head. It would look utterly random to a stranger walking in.

Fourteen years in the *Concord* Fleet meant that those habits were automatic on a starship.

The off-white tabletop in front of him with burn marks, coffee rings, and dried *gunk*, had stretchy nets on each corner.

They held things like his welding laser and clockwork tools down, but kept them at hand.

He was mostly tinkering, anyway. Working on a new waldo arm that he could mount on Suvi's probe. Something to do with his hands while his backbrain dug deep into old memories and raked the muck about until it found what it was looking for.

His nightmares, the last few days, had been spectacular as a result.

The door chime was almost a welcome interruption.

Almost.

Javier took a deep breath, stashed everything under handy nets, and rose.

His back hurt from being hunched over too long on the four-legged stool. Probably time to go do some yoga or something. He was pretty good about maintaining his regular lifting and stretching cycle.

He ran his hand back through his short, black hair and contemplated how much of it was coming in gray now, mostly at his temples, but a little everywhere. He wasn't vain enough to dye it, and many women seemed to think it made him look more distinguished.

Always a good thing, looking good for the women of this crew.

Privately, he made a bet with himself who would be on the other side of that hatch. There were only a few people who would come down here, rather than just call him on the comm to ask a question.

That meant it would be a private conversation.

Another deep breath, finding his calm center, as he approached the hatch.

He unlocked the system and opened it, finding himself staring at her chest. Not hard to do when her breasts were about on a level with his chin. Small ones, to be sure, hiding on top of muscles. Lots of muscles. But breasts.

Djamila Sykora. *Dragoon* of the private service, Strike Corvette *Storm Gauntlet*.

A woman 2.1 meters tall. She towered over Javier by thirty centimeters.

Her brown hair was still worn short to fit inside an armoured lifesuit, buzzed very tight on the sides and spiked into a petite Mohawk on top.

It was still the only thing petite about her.

She had bright, pretty green eyes. They reminded him of Holly, his ex-wife, but he only told her that when he wanted to annoy this woman. Mostly, it was the faint freckles, anyway.

The bone structure in her face wasn't delicate enough to be pretty, but he suspected she could be stunningly beautiful if she ever cared to try. Not that a hardass like Sykora would, unless she was undercover on a grift. Like the Pleasure Dome had been.

Artemis, by Michelangelo.

The only vaguely-female touch was the collection of tiny gold or silver rings, studs, and stones in both ears. Seven on the right. Nine on the left. Nothing through the nose, though.

Javier sized her up, then stepped back and to the side so she could enter.

Today, he couldn't even work up the energy to ogle her ass, or bitch at her intrusion into his personal space.

Just as well. She surprised him by walking to a side wall, crossing her arms, and leaning her weight against it.

That was so out of character for Sykora that Javier had to fight to keep his mouth from falling on the floor.

After all, the woman was a veteran; a bad-ass, former marine of the *Neu Berne* Navy. A close-combat expert of zero-gravity fighting who was commonly referred to as the *Ballerina of Death*.

A woman born with a stick up her ass. And willing to abuse anybody she felt was slacking the slightest amount from their true potential as she saw it.

He would have said they mixed as well as oil and water, but it was frequently petroleum and fire between them.

Javier closed the hatchway and locked it again.

Keeping any of her friends out.

Suvi was in her armed probe and watching from the workbench. If Sykora got out of hand, Javier knew his sidekick would happily shoot the woman.

He walked back to the stool he had been using before, pulled it to the opposite side of the small room, and sat. It put his eyes about at a level with her belly button.

Not that it was visible, but he knew it was there, riding a hard eight-pack of abs. Today, she was in muted gray. Slacks and a button-up overshirt in chambray with a very petite camouflage pattern. The top of a black t-shirt peeked over the highest button.

With a start, Javier realized it was the uniform she had stolen when they snuck aboard *Shangdu*, the resort vessel known as the *Pleasure Dome*. He wondered if that was a conscious choice on her part. And what it said about why she was here.

More unfinished business, at least on her part.

Silence bound them for several seconds.

Javier took another deep breath. Released it.

"Why are you here?" he asked bluntly.

No elegant turn of phrase. No chiding sarcasm. Nothing.

He was tired, and didn't want to deal with the dragoon today. Especially not the scowl on her face.

"*Hammerfield*," she said, finally, in a quiet, alto voice unlike her normal angry bellow.

She was not saying as much as she said.

Javier assaulted her with silence in return.

He could out-patient a hunter like her, probably by orders of magnitude. Patience was his thing.

"It really exists?" she asked, relenting from her harsh stare.

Javier shrugged.

"I told you and Captain Sokolov what I know," he said. "Nastiest piece of orbital chaos I've ever surveyed. And sitting back in the corner, orbiting a small gas giant like one of her moons in a tiny and exceedingly complex LaGrange point, a vessel with a transponder code identifying her as *Hammerfield*. Whether it really is THE *Hammerfield*, I don't know. Won't, until we board her. That was several years ago, and I only memorized so much."

"So it wouldn't be in your old logs?" she asked.

There was something in her voice. Hope?

Her?

What would the High Priestess of Death hope for, in the lost flagship of her own nation's navy, vanished decades before she was born?

The Great War had ended in a collapse so complete that only today was *Neu Berne* anything more than a tourist destination. It was the sort of place rich folks from the *Concord* could go to watch the proud descendants of the warring generation still trying to come to terms with loss.

"You cut up my ship," Javier growled angrily at her. "After you made me kill her. Those logs are written in a symbolic language so dense, only a *Sentience* can unravel them."

Uncertainty crossed Sykora's face.

For a moment, Javier was sure some sort of vampire doppelgänger from a bad sci-fi vid had appeared on his doorstep.

Djamila Sykora didn't know the meaning of the word *uncertain*.

He watched her eyes dart to her left, linger for a second on Suvi's probe, and then return to his face.

Javier saw pain there.

Imposter. Alien. Invader.

Not the dragoon. Not the *Ballerina of Death*.

"I was hoping…" she wavered, uncertain.

Wavered.

Was this woman stoned?

She wasn't a good enough actress to pull this off as a prank.

"What?" Javier said, trying not to snarl at the woman.

If you had told him this morning that his day would go like this…

Sykora took a breath. Held it. Centered herself in the same way he had before opening the door.

Stood back upright, when all her weight had been leaned back. Grounded herself. Pulled her shoulders back and down.

Fixed him with those sharp, emerald eyes. The pain was still there. The uncertainty. The doubts.

"I know you have worked to program your probes for greater autonomy," she said in a voice finding its footing on slippery ice. "I spoke with this one on *Svalbard*. How long would it take you…Is it even possible to augment one of them enough to read those old logs and know if she really is *Hammerfield*?"

"No," Javier said. "It would take me years. We'll be there in less than a week. We have to locate *Hammerfield* and hope nobody else beat us to the punch. Then board her, hoping that the *Sentience* doesn't kill us out of hand, while we figure out a way to reprogram it. Only then will the truth be known, Djamila Sykora."

She sagged, only the tiniest bit. Anybody not watching so closely would have missed it.

What she really wanted to know was if the *Neu Berne* equivalent of King Arthur was out there, waiting for her to come and find him.

Lady Percival, seeking the Grail.

Javier couldn't decide if he hated himself more for dashing this woman's hopes, or not dancing in unholy glee in the process.

And yet, he had promised to kill this woman. One of these days. When it could be made to look like an accident.

Knew that she had made the same vow. The same Arms Race. The unwritten rules in a duel to the death.

And yet…

The conversation with Del about needing this woman.

All possible tomorrows?

Javier stood. It didn't put him at her level, but it put him in her space.

She flinched. Not much. Barely visible.

Enough.

The killer had come in here with all her guards down, hoping her worst enemy would somehow bear good news.

How far they had come from the first time she had shot him.

"I believe it is your old flagship," he said quietly. "I think they knew the end was near, and took her away to prepare for a surprise attack of some sort. Leading the resistance, or something. Why it never happened, nobody knows. We may find out."

He watched Sykora reassemble all her walls. Put them back in place, brick by brick.

Return to that lethal creature he knew as *The Dragoon*.

That comforted Javier, all by itself. They could be proper enemies now, because probably only Captain Sokolov had ever seen this tremendous woman be the least bit vulnerable.

"Why are you doing this, Javier?" she asked.

It wasn't plaintive, nor angry. Inquisitive, perhaps.

Javier nodded in recognition. That was probably the question that had driven her here today. And it had become necessary for her to be vulnerable to ask it. For him to answer it.

Petroleum and fire.

"There is someone I hate more than you, Djamila Sykora," he said simply.

She processed his words, and then nodded.

"And when we destroy them?" she said in a tight voice, eyes boring in on his.

There was no uncertainty in her voice now. Military problem. Military solution. An enemy that needed killing. Nobody better in the galaxy at that task than Djamila Sykora.

Javier felt eternity open up at his feet, a bottomless chasm threatening both of them.

All possible tomorrows?

Javier considered his weariness at the ongoing game, her emotional vulnerability.

All possible tomorrows.

He decided to gamble everything.

"There is a whole galaxy out there, Djamila," he said. "Maybe we'll both fit in it."

He saw doubt in those eyes now, but it was sarcastic. There on the tip of her tongue, wanting to lash him with verbal razors.

As was normal.

"Ha," she said with sharp humor, jutting a jaw at him.

She didn't say anything more. Just turned, walked to the door, and opened it.

She did glance back over her shoulder once, fixing him with a wry smile, a promise that this conversation would resume on some fateful day.

And then she was gone.

Javier let all the air out of his lungs in a loud blow.

He grabbed the stool, slid it over to the worktable, and sat. It wasn't necessary to lock the door at this part. Everything that he had been trying to keep outside was done.

Running lights on Suvi's probe flickered briefly, drawing his eye.

"Why not?" she asked in a petite tone, proving she had been listening very carefully to the byplay. Knowing her, probably scanning both of them with everything she had, monitoring heart rate, respiration, and truth.

Javier understood the core of her question.

Why wasn't he willing to make them promises about "upgrading" the probe so that she no longer had to hide in there, pretending to be nothing more than a dumb-bot set of programmed responses to external stimuli?

"Because I don't want them to even be able to guess what I'm going to do, young lady," he said quietly. "Not until it's too late to stop me."

PART TWO

Zakhar Sokolov looked out over his airy bridge, surrounded by the crew he had hand-picked over the years, having tried to gather the best of the ones who no longer fit their old jobs, or their old navies; frequently for budget cuts, occasionally for being too artistic, too weird, or too much for small fleets with more people seeking employment than jobs were available.

As with most days, Zakhar wore something that very closely approximated the old *Concord* fleet uniform. The fleet that had been his home for twenty years.

Before piracy.

Moss green slacks and a matching, button-up, dress shirt. He had done away with the tie as a daily requirement, but kept his black, leather brogues polished as a reminder.

Who he used to be.

Around him, the bridge crew wore any variety of things, some based on old uniforms from their past, others on whatever deal the purser had been able to swing in terms of cheap, surplus uniforms and gear along the way. Those colors stood out against the laurel green of the various bulkheads, that color midway between green and gray that walls, ceilings, and floors were painted regularly, with white numbers and arrows here and there following conduits.

"Pilot," Zakhar called, waking Piet Alferdinck up from whatever day-dreams the man was enjoying over on his boards. "Confirm time to insertion."

It was there on Zakhar's own screen, but acting like a professional constantly ingrained that habit in his crew. When you were pirates, every day was a struggle against entropy. Doubly so when your ship, the old *Osiris*-class Strike Corvette *Storm Gauntlet*, was on her last legs.

Their last engagement, with the battle frigate *Ajax*, over *Svalbard*, had been a fast one, which was good. *Storm Gauntlet* was enough to take any freighter in the galaxy, but desperately overwhelmed by almost any warship she would encounter.

They had repaired as much of the damage as well as they could. Enough to escape, to flee into the darkness, looking for the place his science officer had hoped they would find an even bigger warship, derelict, but claimable and repairable.

Otherwise, Zakhar would probably be better off selling this old boat to someone else, or even a breaker yard, paying off the crew, and retiring to whatever desk job he thought he could do.

Maybe even go back to his real name and finally tap his retirement pension, sitting in a bank somewhere, slowly earning interest.

What did happily-ever-after taste like?

Zakhar's eye caught his dragoon, Djamila Sykora, just settling into her station, but he refused to think about what the two of them might create, if they didn't have to be pirates anymore.

He was The Captain, and that was a cold, lonely job.

"Thirteen minutes to insertion, Captain," Piet called back.

Zakhar nodded to himself.

"Remember to come out under full cloak," he ordered. "We have no idea how the target will react. I'd rather she not see us at all."

"Roger that," the pilot said.

A side hatch opened on his right, opposite where Djamila was buckling herself in, and the science officer entered.

Djamila was in all gray today. Piet wore a purple tunic and black slacks. Even Mary-Elizabeth Suzuki, the gunner, was in bright green and baby blue.

Javier wore an outfit that was almost an exact copy of Zakhar's, except for the shoes. Javier had soft, blue moccasins today. Still, the *Concord* fleet officer must be running strong in both of them.

They locked eyes for a moment as Javier settled and logged into his boards.

No words passed, but none were needed.

How often did you know ahead of time that you were about to reach a point where the rest of your life would go down a different path from yesterday? The only question now was which of three options they faced.

Success in finding and claiming the lost *Neu Berne* flagship, *Hammerfield*.

Failure, either because it wasn't there, or it was too badly degraded to save them.

Or death, because the ancient warrior vessel took offense to them even being there.

Simple as that.

Around him, everyone settled in, strapped themselves to their chairs, and prepared for their fate to unfold.

"Any final thoughts, Mr. Science Officer?" Zakhar asked, loud enough to include the whole bridge crew in what might have been a simple conversation between old comrades.

"Piet will be paying off on a twenty-drachma bet shortly," Javier replied.

The pilot just shrugged.

"How's that?" Zakhar said.

"That never in his studies or travels has he seen a star system so messy, so complicated," Javier laughed. "So impossible."

Zakhar wasn't sure he believed Javier's stories about the place, but it really didn't matter much at this point. The proof would be in the pudding, as they said. Very shortly.

"All hands," he said into a general comm. "Prepare for insertion and possible combat maneuvering in eight minutes."

Zakhar watched as all stations checked in. Everyone knew the rumors. Knew the score about how badly damaged *Storm Gauntlet* was. She had given as good as she got, but it had still been ugly, protecting the assault shuttle so it could land, while they were all under fire.

Zakhar really looked forward to finding *Ajax* one of these days, and kicking her teeth in to return the favor. And really hurting Walvisbaai Industrial, the multi-system conglomerate that some of the more flamboyant news services might call one of the *Pirate Clans.*

Although never in a place with good libel laws on the books.

Zakhar worked for the Jarre Foundation. Another Clan, if you would.

In the darkness between stellar nations, the law was frequently the man with the bigger warship, the biggest hammer.

And if it was going to be a war between the pirates, the sort of lurid thing that would sell subscriptions, Zakhar wanted the biggest maul available.

A First Rate Galleon would serve that need quite nicely.

Even more than a century old, *Hammerfield* would outclass anything less than a modern cruiser, while still having cargo capacity comparable to the largest of the medium transports, or the smallest of the big bulk jobs that hauled thousands of standard shipping containers between major worlds.

Nobody even made that design anymore, relying today on commercial freighters and dedicated warships, rather than a single ship that mixed the two.

"Piet," Zakhar said. "Bring up screen nine on the main display. Zero transparency. Twenty percent overlay."

They had scanned this system from one jump away, when it was barely possible to resolve it as three stars with the best scanners, using a former probe-cutter's eyes, stolen and welded onto a warship like this one.

Nothing else was really known, given the distance of this

jump, except that they would drop out at around fifty AU, fifty times the distance from Earth to her sun. Even Neptune, the blue ice giant in the Homeworld's system, orbited at thirty AU, so they should be safe enough out here, especially coming out seventy degrees above the ecliptic for the system.

And even then, Javier had warned them to pay attention to their surroundings. Which was frightening in itself, since he rarely ever got serious like that.

Emergence.

Realspace.

Engines primed but off. Shields at minimum only. Electromagnetic cloak fully deployed. Every turret ready to fire.

Riding the gyros and pretending to be an ugly asteroid, as the saying went.

Javier was face down over his boards, studying four different screens and listening to several audio channels through an earpiece.

Complete information overload to anybody but him. Which was why he was *The Science Officer.*

Piet's hands were poised. Mary-Elizabeth's, too. Even Djamila appeared to be holding her breath.

Long, silent minutes passed, everything and everyone hushed and waiting.

"She's still there," Javier said simply.

The sound of a dozen people breathing out was a heavy sigh across the room.

The main display blinked, and changed.

Nayarit Sector, system number 23, in Javier's recollections.

NS005188-753A was at the center, a yellow main sequence star, a G8V, which was only about ten percent larger than that of the homeworld, still the measure everyone used.

At an orbital distance of roughly twelve AU, on a twenty-some degree inclination from the original ecliptic, two smaller stars, *B* and *C*, orbited each other around a common center, a barycenter in open space, not that anything could survive in that LaGrange point indefinitely. At least they were both cooler stars, so the total amount of solar wind wasn't all that bad.

From Javier's recollection, the two stars were about 0.9 and 0.7 times the size of *A*, which made this a complicated triple system, especially since the orbital inclination of the binary suggested that they had been captured fairly recently, perhaps in the last three hundred to five hundred million years at most.

What made it extra fun were the number of gas giants Javier was able to identify and flag on his projection already. Both systems had contained an interesting mix of gas giants, ice giants, and the smaller worlds: both rocky ones close and iceballs farther out.

In this case, it looked like all of the gas giants had somehow managed to be captured, rather than ejected from the combined solar system as all the other planets slowly fell into their various orbital resonance periods in at least two interacting ecliptic planes. The screen showed nine giants so far, with the promise of several more as passive sensors watched and counted.

Zakhar doubted that everything would be stable like this, and that many of these worlds would eventually be eaten or evicted, but that was an issue to occur in millions of years. All he had to worry about today were the possible number of things formerly in the local Oort Cloud, Kuiper Belt, or Scattered Disk.

Quite frankly, there was going to be crap flying everywhere, for a very long time. Even if a rocky world in one of the habitable zones could be identified, terraforming it would be a waste of time during the lifetime of man as a species, unless you wanted to dedicate unholy amounts of ships and men to locating and destroying all of the things that might slam into such a world with enough energy to cause extinction-level events.

There were so many other star systems in this galaxy that weren't assholes to begin with.

Piet actually stood up, pulled out a twenty-drachma bill from a pocket, and walked over to hand it to Javier with a face gone white.

Javier's frog-faced grin said it all.

Nothing less extreme would have brought them here.

One little green dot.

Hammerfield, according to the transponder code faintly calling her name to eternity.

Tucked into the leading LaGrange point, L4, formed by the combination of *A* and the single gravity well of *B* and *C*.

At some point, the dance along multiple ecliptics would probably slam the warship into one of the giants, roaming around like wolves at the edge of the firelight, or their touch would kick the ship entirely out of the system, lost forever in the darkness.

But they were here today. And they had the time to plot a whole series of short hops that would culminate within reach of *Neu Berne*'s last flagship. Trying that in one jump was a recipe for disaster.

"Anybody else here?" Zakhar finally asked, breaking the spell that had wound itself around them with sticky webs.

"Negative, Captain," the science officer said professionally, which told Zakhar how far down the rabbit hole Javier had gone in his mind.

He was never formal unless he had to be. Or he forgot where he was and fell into the old ways.

"Then you have the bridge," Zakhar ordered. "Primary crew stand down for now. We'll have food delivered when you are ready, Javier."

Javier's look told Zakhar how much sarcasm was on the tip of his tongue, but he held his silence.

They both knew that this place held the sort of mysteries that would keep him glued to his station until the caffeine stopped working.

Zakhar rose and considered some coffee himself and maybe a little dessert as a treat.

Now, the hard part would start.

Djamila powered her electronic book reader down and closed the brown, leather cover. It was technically an antique at this point, fifty-one years old, but it had belonged to her father as a child, before he gave it to her as a graduation present, and it had been built to last at least another century.

She traced soft fingertips on the faded brown leather, fifteen centimeters by twenty-five, and thought about the past. Her past.

Her world's past.

They had been here in-system for one hundred and thirteen hours now. Still sitting out at the very top edge of the system, looking down from a dizzying height at everything moving, like a giant mobile that had hung over her crib.

Djamila had already studied everything there was to know about the *Hammerfield*.

Class specifications, interior systems diagrams, everything. There hadn't been time to transform deck plans from her records into a full immersion video, but she had memorized most of the layout. That part didn't concern her.

No, she had been reading a history of the war itself. One she had never read during her military student days.

It had been written some years after the war, by a woman

who had been a mid-level officer serving the Admiralty Staff at the time of *The Surrender*.

That moment when the government itself had collapsed, and the survivors were too weary to push on any further, thirty-nine years of near-continuous warfare having apparently been enough, even for a warrior culture like hers had been.

It wasn't there on the page, what Djamila sought today. It wouldn't be.

As near as she knew, the secrets she wanted had probably never left this very star system, interred forever under alien suns.

At the same time, the words she read had been written when the memories of those days were fresh. Before the rise of the great legends and lies about betrayals and heroes gone into hiding, like Arthur gone to *Avalon* with Excalibur in his hand. Geoffrey of Monmouth would have been proud of the lies and myths her parents' generation had concocted.

She had heard those stories enough growing up that she had believed them.

Not anymore.

High Command had gambled everything on a major offensive and been mousetrapped.

Slaughtered.

It wasn't as bad as that final battle at *A'Nacia*, five hundred years ago, but it had broken *Neu Berne*'s back psychologically.

Hammerfield had managed to escape the wreckage and return home, undamaged. After a quick stop to pick up supplies and Admiral Ericka Steiner, head of the Admiralty itself, the warship had leapt into the darkness and never been heard from again.

Even today, any records of that mission were classified. Missing. Taken away by official men.

But not on *Neu Berne* or one of the *Union* worlds. Not even *Balustrade*, the immortal enemy.

No.

The *Concord* had swept it all up, six years later, when it flexed its newly-won hegemony across the near galaxy. Ridden in and taken control. All records simply disappeared except what was written down later by the people who knew, who remembered the truth, what little of it there was to know.

After that, only legends.

Now, eighty-five years later, Djamila Sykora looking for the warship, the weapon, that held the truth.

Would she find Excalibur?

Did she even want to?

PART FOUR

Important events should be treated as such. Javier's grandmother had always told him that as a child.

As a result, he had shaved off several days of ugly, salt-and-pepper stubble from his chin. A shower with real water, rather than his usual pass through the low-power sonic cleaner. Aftershave that made him smell like his grandfather. Clothing without any stains, even if he had to go clear to the bottom of the drawer for the dungarees.

Gray fit his mood, anyway, so he wore the charcoal pants, with a marbled gray raglan pullover with black sleeves, and the soft blue moccasins he habitually wore when he wasn't leaving the ship.

He had taken the time for a quick haircut. Javier didn't figure he had been this spiffy even for dates in a while.

And he was there early for the meeting, prepped, and supplied with really good coffee. Sascha and Hajna were there, as was Sykora, and Afia Burakgazi.

Captain Sokolov entered the primary conference room like it was full of snakes. It wasn't.

Hell, they weren't any of them even doppelgängers, last time he had checked. Personally in three cases. Visually with Sykora.

There was no way in hell he was getting that intimate with the dragoon.

Nope. Javier, seated at the far end of the long, pseudo-grain-laminate table, sat and sipped coffee from his mug, the one he had found in the wardroom. The one that someone, somewhere, had picked up at a Merankorr brothel gift shop. The one which, based on the amount of hot coffee inside, would currently show a beautiful young woman with green hair, and no clothing north of her belly-button.

Because he could.

He hadn't bought the damned thing. Just recognized it on a shelf in the wardroom for what it was and kept it. Because he had owned something similar, a long time ago.

On Javier's immediate right was Afia, a short, skinny engineer with a heart-shaped face, dark green eyes, and the willingness and ability to beat up men twice her size in bars, though you would never guess it from the demure way she rested her chin on her laced fingers and smiled. Those women were always the most dangerous ones, anyway.

Her ancestors had originally come from somewhere in southeast Asia on the homeworld. Roughly between what used to be China and Indonesia, back in the old days. Her skin was darker, more golden, than the Chinese Diaspora, but not the red-brown of Javier's.

Across from Afia was Sascha Koç, one of Sykora's two pathfinder babes, the scouts she relied upon in hostile territory. Sascha was a short, Slavic brunette with lush hips and an amazing alto singing voice. Today she was in her usual field uniform: pants and button-up tunic with a gray and maroon splotch pattern apparently designed to vanish shipboard. Javier couldn't see it, but they believed.

Diagonal from Sascha was her counterpart, Hajna Flores, the lanky, Anglo blond with legs that seemed to go on forever and were born to tango. Like Sascha, Hajna dressed for war, although she had added a floral-scented something to her morning routine today.

Both women were card sharps of the first order, the kind

that usually just about broke even playing with Javier; whereas the three of them cleaned out anybody else wanting to play.

Hajna might be the smarter of the pair, but that was like judging which day was nicer. They were both wicked brilliant women. And dangerous, which he appreciated.

Sykora waited at what would be Sokolov's right hand when he sat. That was pretty much her reserved seat in any meeting he was attending. Like the pathfinders, she wore the steel and maroon that was supposed to hide you against gray walls.

Javier assumed it had something to do with inducing motion sickness in anyone watching the optical illusion of the spots moving for long enough. Fortunately, his stomach was made of sterner stuff.

Still, Sokolov blinked as he sat.

"I would have expected you to take Ilan, Javier," he said as he settled.

"That man has not certified on combat EVA," Javier retorted with a knowing grin.

Sokolov nodded, then turned sharply to stare at Afia, quite possibly the quietest person in the room. Most rooms.

To her credit, the woman shrugged nonchalantly and smiled a wicked, evil grin at the man.

Some people would have taken a different lesson from their adventures on *Meehu Platform*. Afia had apparently decided to become more dangerous. At this rate, she might end up on Sykora's combat team, and not down in the engineering spaces.

Of course, as many times as he got drug along on assaults in his job as science officer, maybe this ship needed a dedicated combat engineer. Weirder things had happened, especially with this crew.

"So what do we know?" Sokolov turned back to Javier, all serious and military shit now.

"Nothing," Javier retorted.

"Nothing?" Sokolov was surprised. "We've been here a week."

"You said *Know*," Javier snarked. "I have any number of pet theories to test."

"Oh, fine." Sokolov settled himself more comfortably and visibly prepared for war with his science officer. "Top three."

"As near as memory serves, she hasn't moved in six years," Javier ticked off his fingers. "I'm hoping that means that she was parked there by someone who knew what they were doing."

"And the warship has not moved on its own, subsequent," Sokolov observed.

"Which brings me to my second theory," Javier continued. "The *Sentience* is dead, the ship is disabled, or she was ordered to remain there until someone came for her."

"I have very little experience with *Sentient* ships," Sokolov said. "What are the odds?"

"They tend to come off the assembly line extremely linear," Javier replied. "Black and white. Like bright five-year-olds. What happens with their first crew, their first captain, tends to set their personality. I got lucky with my probe-cutter. Captain Ayumu Ulfsson was one hell of a man and set her on the right path. Who knows with *Neu Berne*? Especially a flagship."

They both glanced quickly at Sykora, but she shrugged tightly, silently. Not out of her depth, but out of her expertise and willing to let the experts speculate unless asked a direct question.

Javier always forgot how professional the woman could be when they didn't have to argue.

"Risks?" Sokolov asked.

"Eighty-five years of boredom," Javier said. "Think how crazy you'd be, left in solitary confinement for that long."

"Can we fix any of those issues?" Sokolov asked. "Dead, disabled, or crazy?"

"Dead could mean a simple power failure took her offline," Javier said. "Or maybe a lunatic smashed the right boards and killed it. I can reprogram it from scratch in that case, given enough time and access to the right hardware and software backups, both of which are hopefully stored close at hand."

Sykora twitched.

Coming from her, a scream in a darkened opera house would have been less disturbing. Javier could tell she wanted to inject something, probably bilious, into the conversation, but she held her silence.

Sokolov saw it as well. He glanced, but she shook her head.

"You told me, when we first captured you, Javier, that you couldn't do that," Sokolov observed dryly.

"No," Javier replied with a hard smile. "I told you to go to hell. It wouldn't be an easy or quick task. And would require a good chunk of the engineering crew for at least a month, if we have to code up from a declarations block. But it can be done. I've been practicing on my probes, and in a year, have gotten them about as smart as a cat. She would end up programming a good chunk of her own personality once we started."

"Okay," Sokolov breathed out, apparently willing to let that one go, unaware of how much of a lie it was. "What about crazy?"

Javier leaned back in his chair and took a long drink of coffee.

Sokolov was directly across from him, with the four women warriors between them. Five pairs of eyes fixed on him. Green, blue, brown, green, brown, from his right.

"That's why Afia and not Ilan," Javier said. "I'm proposing a combat insertion. *Storm Gauntlet* stays cloaked and deploys Del in the Assault Shuttle. He gets us to a certain point, maybe fifty kilometers out, and drops us. We EVA over and hopefully board her with no issue."

"Or?" Sokolov asked.

"Or she kills us and then goes after Del," Javier replied. "You'll be able to get away, because her scanners aren't likely good enough to penetrate a modern cloak. What you do at that point isn't my concern."

Captain Sokolov looked at the other four individually, until each nodded, Sykora last.

"Is it worth it?" Sokolov asked in a heavy, tired voice.

Javier tapped a finger on the tabletop.

"As I told Sykora, I've found someone I hate more than any of you," he rasped. "I refuse to spend the rest of my life looking over my shoulder for an assassin. These people only understand power and fear. Wealth gives them power to inflict fear on others. That offends me. Badly."

He took another sip of coffee, getting close to the really good, caramel sludge at the bottom of his mug, and fixed the captain with his stare.

"Zakhar Sokolov," Javier ground the words out. Witnesses, and all that. "I told you I was willing to start with a blank screen here. Old wounds and slights will be forgotten. We will be partners in this endeavor. I intend to dedicate my life to destroying those people. Burning their cities, pulling down the ruins, and salting the earth. Scipio Africanus the Younger. That sort of thing. If it gets me killed here, then those are the risks. I've talked to these four and spelled it out for them. They're here."

"I always thought Navarre was crazy," Sokolov said with a wry smile. "Turns out Aritza is even worse."

Javier nodded grimly as the four women warriors around him got a chuckle out of the captain's words.

You have no idea.

BOOK EIGHTEEN: DERELICT

Suvi was in her big probe today, the armed one with the way-bigger memory block to store movies and books. Loaded for a vacation of at least three weeks before she had to loop.

To humans, the sensors on the face of her flyer apparently made it look like a big gray eyeball, floating in space. When she deployed the popup turret from the bottom, it got vaguely obscene.

Around her, Suvi tracked the other five humans getting ready for deep space. All that remained was to lock helmets in place, check everything, and transition to onboard systems.

Unlike the normal skinsuits they might wear for short jaunts, the humans had strapped themselves into anonymous, gray EVA suits. Heavier. Bulkier. Semi-armoured.

Backpacks with pressurized systems for directed flight. Gear bags and equipment belts. Spare oxygen tanks and power packs. Toolkits.

Each was equipped with on-board plumbing attachments that took some getting used to, apparently, to listen to Javier bitch. But Javier liked to complain about things. It was his nature. Of course, it was a little easier for females in that department.

Not that she had ever had physical form requiring such shenanigans, but she could research it, and commiserate with them.

Silently, of course. She didn't really exist.

To make things even funnier, at least to an AI in her own pocket spaceship, the suits had some level of armored reinforcement, so people tended to waddle awkwardly when they moved. Like they had drunk themselves right up at the edge of too tipsy to operate heavy equipment safely.

Ugly, gray penguins.

Well, everyone except Djamila Sykora. She moved in her suit with a grace that would have embarrassed many professional athletes. Suvi finally understood the term: *a Natural.*

And they weren't really anonymous as they prepared. Sykora was a head taller than anyone and had three weapons in holsters: both hips and under her left arm, where everyone else only had one on their dominant hip. Javier was broader than Hajna in the shoulders and body. And Sascha was bulkier than Afia.

That would be useful as Suvi helped them transit deep space, flying like a herding dog working vaguely-recalcitrant sheep, if her videos were accurate. The gear bag Javier had prepared for her to carry made her feel almost like a locomotive pulling a single, heavy car through space. It was two meters long, by a third of that square, and weighed forty kilograms in gravity, but Javier had explained that he was prepared for almost any task with it handy.

A sound drew her attention, so she rotated herself around to bring her primary video pickup in line.

Delridge Smith ambled loosely down the set of steps from his flight deck to the big cargo bay.

Del stared right at her and winked, as if they were sharing some joke.

Suvi never knew with the pilot. He was much older than the rest of the crew, and much looser. Today, he had clipped his white beard short, maybe only a number fifteen length on the trimmer, while he kept the white hair on his head around a ten. Olfactory sensors suddenly picked up an alcohol-based volatile trace, but it was a perfume of some sort, and not bourbon.

Coconut, according to the onboard spectrograph, whatever that meant.

Like every day, he was in gray cargo pants and a floral shirt. Hawaiian, per her onboard encyclopedia. Off-peach with white parrot silhouettes. Not even the weirdest one he owned.

"Roughly fifty kilometers out," Del announced. "Holding a lateral motion and on autopilot. So what do I do if it spots you and starts to move?"

"Run like hell," Javier said. "Get rocks, moons, or planets between you and it and hope it either loses you, or loses interest. She can splatter you from here if she wants to. I'm hoping we're not a threat, this small and this far away. *Storm Gauntlet* might have provoked a reaction."

"Kid, you're crazy," Del said. "But I'll give you credit for brass."

He stopped and looked around at the rest.

"Ladies, if we all get killed today, it has been my pleasure flying with you."

Everyone made insulting comments. Afia included a rude, universal gesture as well.

Del laughed, saluted, and tromped back up the stairs. A hatch latched shut with the sound of a vault door.

Suvi watched Javier step close to the dragon lady.

"When we latch down, you're in charge," he said. "The probe knows the basic hand language you use with your team. Everyone maintains complete radio silence until we're all inside, either here or there. If anyone has an emergency, they return here on their own. Any questions?"

There were none, but that was ignorance, not confidence.

Nobody but Javier had any experience with a *Sentient* starship. Well, not counting her, but she found most of her cousins to be annoyingly stuffy, boring shits. Really bad conversationalists.

Humans were way preferable for that sort of thing.

One by one, the team locked their helmets down. External status lights cycled up to green for everyone else to see.

You never knew when maybe something was going wrong and you passed out before you knew it. Helpful if your suit yelled for assistance for you. Humans were really fragile creatures, that way.

And then silence. Everybody trapped in their own, private world. At least she had planned ahead and had enough music for a millennia aboard, plus whatever she might write between now and then.

Suvi went into the tiny airlock with the dragon lady first.

That made sense. Put the two best flyers out in vacuum before anyone else.

The confined space hissed weirdly on her audio pickups as pumps sucked the room empty.

Ready? Sykora signaled silently.

Suvi had a ring of signaling lights below her main sensor grid. She cycled a muted, Kelly green, clockwise pattern, and watched the giant woman nod.

Push came to shove, Suvi could turn the lights into a Times Square scrolling marquee, but she wasn't supposed to be that smart, especially not around the dragon-lady.

And then silence. The outer door of the airlock opened towards them, revealing an eternity of stars dancing mutely.

Suvi bounced outward on her gyros and micro thrusters, just enough to get three meters from the hatch, so she could play lifeguard with her Santa Claus bag of goodies trailing behind her.

She watched Sykora grab a doorframe and pivot herself outward like the ballerina she was called. The dragoon let go of the ship so perfectly she didn't move.

Wow.

Then the woman reached out with one finger and pushed just enough to drift backwards at a pace that snails would have appreciated. It was almost like watching paint dry.

Pretty impressive, especially for an organic.

The hatch closed outwards to them, sealed, and there was nothing to do but watch. Or passively scan on all frequencies available, with a spectrum bandwidth that would have made anybody but Javier nervous.

Hammerfield was over there. A transponder signal quietly chirping on channel eighty-three. Hash and junk on several other channels that Suvi decided must be gas giants gossiping to themselves under the triple solar wind.

She didn't have any memories of being here before, but Javier hadn't had any excuse before now to access her old drives, other than to confirm that the files were all securely stored on her old memory core, itself stashed away in a vacuum-sealed storage box in engineering.

One of these days, she would get to look at her old picture albums.

Sascha and Hajna came out second. Not quite as graceful as the dragon lady, but well above average. The sort of skill that only came with extensive practice in a zero-g environment.

Afia and Javier were last. Suvi would have said graceful, but she had just watched two experts and a dragon-lady give lie to that observation.

She suppressed the urge to bark out loud before she started herding, then realized that nobody would hear her, as long as she didn't display it on one of her boards or transmit it over radio, so she gave one loud *woof,* just to set the tone in her own head.

Each suit was programmed with coordinates and burn cycles, but too much of it was estimation, and an expectation that the individual pilot would exercise terminal control. Or rely on one of the lifeguards if something went wrong.

One by one, they slowly began to move, accelerating at a comfortable, predictable pace, with fifty kilometers of space to cover but no major deadline, since these suits were good for up to two weeks of average use.

Suvi went last. She fired up a DeManx Symphony, Number Forty-three, from the sixty-third century. The late *Corporate*

Wars period had produced some lovely orchestral music, not like the grand choral pieces of the early *Pocket Empires Era*, starting in the sixty-sixth century. But of the crew, only Piet Alferdinck, the pilot, had any true appreciation of music history anyway.

Hopefully, one of these days, she would get to discuss it with him.

PART TWO

IT HAD STARTED out as a point of light, just emerging from the darkness. Djamila had watched it resolve itself into an object, a gleaming, metallic form somewhere between a longsword and the Caduceus of Hermes. It looked organic to her, living in a period where naval architecture had gone to straight lines and geometric symmetry.

Overall, *Hammerfield* was just over a kilometer long, with a beam ratio of only thirteen to one. Stubbier than *Storm Gauntlet*, which made sense, since their vessel was a dedicated warship, where space was at a premium, while this relic was a galleon, armed with a variety of medium-sized guns, turreted on all four sides, wrapped around gargantuan cargo holds.

Storm Gauntlet had three big-gun twin turrets on her top deck, with point-defense weapons all around her. Sleek and deadly, like a knife, rather than a sledgehammer.

It did not look like a tomb, but Djamila wasn't fooled. As remote and isolated as this system was, she couldn't imagine someone parking the ship here and taking further flight in something smaller, something weaker. There had been very few warships larger than *Hammerfield* in that era, which made this one all the more important to whoever had her.

That meant that they had come here and never left.

Died here.

Djamila reviewed her mental list of the sorts of causes of death that she should prepare for. Sudden plague vectors that might still be viable, even after this period. Violent civil war among the crew. Accidental decompression, the kind that would kill some and isolate the rest in small, personal mausoleums from which they could never escape.

For the briefest moment, she entertained the exotic fiction of survivors, or the offspring thereof, somehow having managed to make it this far, like some dime-novel space fantasy. Unlikely, but still possible. One of the reasons why she was so well armed.

Survivors today would most likely be feral creatures, not civilized humans.

She took a deep breath to settle herself, tasting the flat, metallic tang of the recycling plant's air. The onboard sensors were all green, but Djamila dialed up the humidity three percent anyway, hoping it would improve the taste in her mouth.

She listened as her thrusters began to taper down, blowing forward over her shoulders and around her hips to slow her. It had been two hundred and eight minutes, and they were very close to the ancient warship. It had resolved itself into a wall of steel.

The Last Flagship.

She wasn't sure what she would have done, had the vessel begun to move as they approached, or opened fire.

Died gloriously in battle, she supposed. Everyone had always expected that of her.

Nothing more.

No grand accomplishments, save to make the Valkyries themselves jealous when they came for her.

Djamila let her backbrain consider what legacy she really wanted to leave, in a galaxy where violent death was not necessarily a job requirement. She had never really thought about it, but this ancient tomb spoke to her on very unconscious levels.

What we leave behind.

Silence. She was motionless relative to *Hammerfield*. Perhaps thirty meters away, drifting with the ship through space, pulled by unseen tides of solar gravity.

She looked over at Javier. He didn't know the hand language well enough for complicated conversations, but had enough of the basics.

Next step? she asked.

He gave her a thumbs-up and began to close on the bow of the ship. The man had obviously studied the schematics she had provided, at least well enough to locate the forward crew airlock. She signaled the others to follow, and drew her right-hand pistol.

Djamila had visions of small, armed automatons on the hull, popping out to engage and destroy boarding parties in exactly this circumstance. She was prepared to kill them.

Perhaps she was a touch crazy, as well.

But better to be paranoid unnecessarily, rather than complacent and wiped out.

PART THREE

Javier let visions of avarice dance in his background as he silently came to rest against the hull of the ancient, *Neu Berne* warship. For years, looting this beast had been a significant chunk of his retirement planning. The sort of thing that would generate enough cash that he could live on a private beach with his own, personal bartender for the rest of his days.

And now? Vengeance.

You wanna play rough, assholes? I'll show you what rough really tastes like.

People born rich never understand what poverty does to someone. How it shapes their willingness to color outside the lines. They've never worried about paying the rent every month, and all the things they might have to do to get there.

Javier let the scowl own his face for a while. There was nobody in a position to look into his polarized helmet and see just what demon had possessed him.

Safer this way.

Javier Aritza was kind of a clown. That was okay. Eutrupio Navarre was a cold, hard killer. Even Navarre might have blanched and recoiled right now.

Hammerfield's exterior was polished clean, a sharp, blue-steel, alloy finish that told him the nav shields were rarely activated, letting the triple solar wind play across the hull like a high-grit sandpaper.

In front of him, the airlock controls.

Javier glanced back to make sure Suvi and Sykora were still with him. Suvi's gear bag had a prybar strong enough to force the door, if necessary. Sykora had the muscles to make that happen.

Javier set his guidance systems to hold him steady as he worked, little puffs of gas that would fly all directions.

He reached out a gloved hand and pressed the button to open the keypad. Nothing happened. No power? Welded shut by time and errant plasma?

Javier reached down to his belt and pulled out the most primitive tool a spaceman ever carried: a flat piece of polished steel, three millimeters thick and twenty-five wide, ground down to a chisel tip. A bit of string attached it to the sheath, so it wouldn't fly away if he dropped it. Because he had *never* done that.

Javier activated the magnets in his boots and left hand to give him some extra leverage against the hull, and slipped the edge of the tool into the space around the panel.

Torque brought out the muscles in his back.

In space, there was no rewarding pop as whatever was holding it gave way, but he could feel it in his hands. He sheathed his chisel and studied the controls revealed. Ten-key pad. Radio buttons.

There we are: Big red emergency override.

Javier couldn't imagine that the beast inside, that grand, ancient dragon called a *Sentience*, might have missed their approach, even as stealthy as they had been, but pushing this button would most certainly wake it up.

Knock, knock.

Javier pushed the button until he felt it stop. It lit as it went in, which was a promising sign. He had feared that all power would be off, and they would have to pry the hatch open after all.

More lights came on. A string of them in white outlined the

airlock hatch. Javier smiled as the door slowly receded into the hull on hinges, revealing an airlock chamber large enough for ten or fifteen good friends to fill.

He wasn't entirely sure what all the hand signals Sykora gave him meant, but her intent on going first was obvious. As was his willingness to let her.

Always put well-armed, crazy chicks on point where they might stop all the hordes of hell in their tracks. Sykora was like that.

At least the airlock was internally lit. Bright, white lights revealed a clean interior. The slightest rime of frost as a few traces of air bled out, so hopefully there was atmospheric pressure inside after all this time.

More hand signals. Hajna joined Sykora in the box while the rest of them were apparently supposed to wait outside. Whatever.

The hatch slid ominously closed, a bank vault that slowly sealed shut.

Long minutes passed.

Javier found himself inspecting a sensor pod nearby, his primary nerdiness coming to the fore when the situational stress got too much. The pod was worn and pitted. Probably blind after all this time. Certainly, it didn't emit any signals he could pick up.

And Suvi hadn't made any indication that the dragon might be waking.

The outer hatch lit up and began to cycle again, a humongous Venus Flytrap waiting its next customer.

Given the space, Javier entered and signaled the three women to join him inside. He pressed the big, green button on the inner wall when everyone was set.

A sign lit up above the button. Javier read German, which had been the universal standard message for airlocks of all nations, dating back thousands of years, but the message was written in eleven other languages in smaller print below, just in case.

Warning: Gravplates activating.

The direction of the text provided your context, if you had somehow gotten confused about the shape of the warship around you.

The plates powered up slowly, giving even the most distracted fool time to realize what was happening and get his feet pointed in the right direction. At the same time, more lights came on and Javier could feel a rumbling hiss through his boots as air got pumped into the chamber.

All good signs. Assuming no alien monster from his worst nightmares was standing on the other side of the inner hatch when it opened.

The door cycled out into the hallway.

Okay, this monstrous nightmare was not unexpected.

Sykora.

She had depolarized her faceplate, so he could see her grimace inside. She wasn't scowling much more than normal. And had a pistol in either hand, but that was usual for her as well.

Suvi went out first, sliding around the Amazon and taking up a station overhead. Javier *felt* the ping she unleashed, clear down in his bones.

NOTHING was sneaking up on those two women.

He joined them in the hall, along with Sascha, Hajna, and Afia, snug as a bug in a rug.

External sensors showed everything here in the tolerable range. Oxygen/nitrogen mix close enough for government work. No dangerous traces underneath.

Colder than snot out in the hallway, though. Ambient hallway temperature four degrees and atmospheric equivalent of twenty-five hundred meters above sea level.

Camping in the Northern Rockies, back on Earth, in winter. Still, tolerable.

Javier reached up with both hands and pressed the buttons to open his helmet. The buttons were located on either side of the forehead, where Sykora had obviously ground off her horns with a disk sander at some point in the past.

The faceplace itself was three pieces that came together like a fishbowl with nearly invisible seams. They popped open now and retracted, kinda rolling up like shades, down right, down left, and up center, leaving the backpiece behind his ears and the helmet crown atop his skull.

Smelled dry in here. Which was way better than smelling like dead people. Visions of Egyptian mummy movies had plagued him for days.

Javier didn't bother with a weapon at this point. Not with as many armed women as he had close by.

Instead, he opened up the comm and set it to scanning all the frequencies for a signal. Most people never realized how much noise a *Sentient* starship made, controlling remotes and sub-systems. You had to have owned one.

Or been one, in Suvi's case. He figured she would say something if she needed to, witnesses be damned. Still, better to check.

"Probe. Access Command Node," he said aloud, perpetuating the myth that the big eyeball was about as smart as a rabbit. "Confirm status."

"Conditions nominal," she replied in the most amazingly droll and bored voice he had ever heard her use.

So yeah, safe, for now.

Javier tapped his helmet and nodded to the four organic women, indicating that they were safe to open up their faceplates as well. Emergency systems could always slam them shut in an eyeblink if something went wrong.

They all emerged from their plastic chrysalis shells and sniffed.

"Where's first?" Afia asked.

She was an engineer first and hadn't drawn a weapon, unlike the other three women. Four. Suvi's pop-down turret was deployed and ready to go.

"We have lights, power, and atmosphere tolerable to human standards," Javier mused aloud.

He looked around the hallway for the first time.

Human standards. Naval architecture, so straight lights, square corners, gray paint, strange pipes and conduits that popped out of walls occasionally, ran a ways, and then popped back in.

Ugly.

There was a reason cruise ships spent so much time and money on hiding all of that behind a Hollywood set.

"I had planned engineering first," Javier replied to Afia. "Just in case. But I think we can do the bridge first and see what we know."

He caught Sykora's eye. She nodded to him.

Man, that woman did not understand poker. Not one bit. Everyone else here would have cleaned her out in about four hands.

It was obvious she wanted to know what had happened to the crew. Why the great mystery? Where was King Arthur hiding?

"Which way?" Sykora asked in a cold, tight voice, like ice chipped off a concrete dam in winter.

"Forward stairs," he replied, mildness itself.

"That's eleven decks," Afia whined lightly. "Why not the lift?"

Javier started to say something, but Sykora got there first.

"Do you want to be trapped in a lift with a potentially hostile *Sentience* controlling it?" the big Amazon asked in a cruel voice.

"Oh," the tiny engineer thought about it. "Yeah, no."

The dangerous women apparently telepathically flipped coins and organized themselves. Javier and Afia ended up in the middle of the line, with Hajna on point, followed by Sykora, and Suvi's probe flying overhead. Sascha brought up the rear.

The stairwell, when they got there, showed all the imagination of the rest of the ship. Three-and-a-half-meter-wide treads, enough for three people to move at once, or two in armoured suits. Up a half-deck, landing, half-turn, up the next. Motion sensing lights at regular intervals.

A little over half of the lights even worked, at least enough to show the way as they entered the square column.

Javier was glad Afia was in even worse condition than he

was. He stayed in shape with yoga and regular weight-lifting. The engineer just had youth on her side.

The other three were the kind of people that did hikes on *Storm Gauntlet* where they put on fifteen kilo packs and walked every hallway, every other day.

Boring, but they weren't wheezing after six decks, either.

At least nothing jumped out at them.

Javier ignored Sykora's smirk as they got to Deck Four and stood around catching their breath. He felt like a forty-year-old man today. And no, he was not taking up running so he could keep up with the kids.

Deep breath. Angry growl.

Let's do this.

There was absolutely no reason to put the bridge on Deck Four. When you sailed on water, it made sense, since your captain needed to be high enough to look around and direct things.

Javier supposed that *Neu Berne* had just never gotten over that. *Concord* ships put it as close to the center of the ship as they could, on the assumption that since it was really hard to actually blow a ship up, you frequently had to stab it to death with beams that acted like ice picks.

Maybe those bastards just wanted everybody in shape from climbing too many damned stairs on a daily basis. Looking at Sykora, he could see that.

You didn't get a bottom that perfect sitting on it at a work station.

"Probe," Javier called. "Map, please. Deck Four, centered on us."

Sykora started to say something, but subsided at the scowl he directed her way.

Yes, I was aware that you have memorized the entire layout of this ship and could probably tell me the room numbers as we go. Unless I plan to crack your skull open and suck your brains out with a straw, princess, I need to see it as well.

That thought had its advantages.

Suvi projected onto the deck below them, saving him the

extra step of orienting himself. Another reason he had asked his most favorite woman, and not his least.

Again, stupid design decision, to put it barely a fifth of the way back from the bow, but it saved him having to walk very far from here.

And still, nothing had jumped out at them, or spoken to them.

If he didn't know better, he would have thought this was a simpler ship. Like *Storm Gauntlet*. Automated to a high degree, but not self-directing. Follow orders and nothing more.

Or the dragon was sprawled out on his horde of gold coins like the ancient story, just waiting for them to enter his lair.

And Javier, without a ring of invisibility.

They tromped on. There was nothing silent and sneaky about this group, except maybe how much firepower the four women could bring to bear in the flash of an eye. Or eyeball, in Suvi's case.

The hatch to the bridge was definitely not standard naval architecture. If it had been, it would have been that plain gray-green everything else was, and standard height and width. This one was an extra fifty centimeters wider, a whole meter taller, and banded with extra straps of a golden metal running vertically in three places.

Like it really wanted to be a bank vault when it grew up. Heavy, imposing, secure. As if the Admiral on the other side was expecting an enemy assault force to board and try to storm the bridge itself.

That, at least, sounded like something *Neu Berne* would do.

Javier found the three camera sensors in the frame: two at eye level on each side, and one overhead. The little lights next to the lenses were out. Hopefully, the dragon wasn't watching.

Like all starships, there was a panel on the right. Humans tended to be right-handed, so it was standard. If the *Sentience* was watching, he would let you in after he identified you. If something went wrong, you could key in a security code to prove who you were. If the *Sentience* went off-line, theoretically you could override things from here.

"*Hammerfield*, open the hatch, please," Javier said in a firm, polite voice. In German, even.

What the hell, it might even work.

It was that or *Open Sesame.*

Nothing happened.

Unlike the airlock, there was no emergency override button here. And a ten-key pad with only a trillion options to try.

This was why he brought Afia. Beyond surrounding himself with beautiful, competent women. Although, one should never overlook that.

"Afia," he turned to her with a smile, pointing at the box. "Would you be so kind as to open that so we can get to the door control circuits?"

Her gear was tucked into custom sleeves and pockets on the outside of her suit, where she could get at them by touch alone when working. She pulled something from her left thigh and something from her belt and tapped metal on metal on the casing while she kneeled down to get her nose almost up against it, like an insurance specialist trying to identify a forged painting.

The other women went into a defensive array, guns in every direction and hostility like an ugly fog boiling off of them.

However, Sykora almost seemed to be fidgeting, which was completely unlike her.

This was one of the few times he didn't mind. Creator only knew what a bored and desperate *Sentience* might throw at them. Nobody had stun weapons in hand right now.

Afia had the case off in seconds, without using a prybar. Another reason he had brought her.

Inside, electronic guts that didn't mean all that much to Javier, but apparently were a roadmap to an engineer. She studied it for a few seconds and then looked up at him.

"It's unlocked," she said simply. "I can open it anytime you want."

"I'll cover it," Sykora barked out.

"No, you will not," Javier replied.

"Why not?"

She rounded on him, angry, overbearing, willing to use her greater size to whatever affect it might have.

None. He wasn't going to budge.

"Because you are too emotionally involved, Dragoon," Javier said. "You are not tactical right now."

That got through to her.

She snarled at him, and then blinked.

Amazingly, the Amazon woman holstered both pistols with a curse of frustration.

"Damn it," she growled. "Damn you. And you're right."

She tilted her head down and looked both ways up the hallway.

"Probe, you cover the door," she said. "Can I watch?"

Javier nodded up at her, at the anguish he saw in those eyes. As much as he wanted to hate this woman, as much joy as destroying her would bring him, he needed her intact. Not just now. Maybe for a long time.

However long it took to win a war with pirates.

Let the universe sort it out after that.

Javier looked at both pathfinders, made sure they nodded back at him. Suvi was faster than even Sykora, if somebody needed to be killed when that door opened. Sykora could probably still draw and shoot faster than anyone holding a pistol.

"Open it up," he said to Afia.

She nodded and reached out with her right hand. Something clicked and the whole vault door began to move sideways into the left-hand wall.

PART FOUR

AFIA DIDN'T HAVE any dog in this fight.

The dragoon was a hard-ass professional, every waking moment, but she was also living in a galaxy where disdainful men tended to run things, so the giantess had to be twice as good as any man at her job to even be considered adequate. *Storm Gauntlet* ran a lot less sexist because that woman wouldn't take any shit from any man, and wouldn't allow any man to become a problem or a predator.

Hell, if you looked at it that way, *Neu Berne* itself, then or now, was way more socially advanced than most of the others. Even *Concord* folk really only tended to talk a good game, but didn't always deliver, Captain Sokolov being a notable exception.

Javier, as compared to Sykora or Sokolov, was a total goofball most of the time, but he was never selfish, in bed or on duty. And that went a long way in Afia's book.

"Open it up," Javier kinda growled, but his anger wasn't aimed at her.

Sykora was in the wrong on this one. She was only here because nobody would tell her she couldn't be, the only *Bernian* in the entire crew, making maybe the biggest discovery in the culture's history.

Afia reached out and triggered the mechanical linkage that the computer would have brought in-line, had she known to just push the *Open* button. None of them had thought to ask. At least nobody had suggested blasting the door open.

She was pretty sure there was enough firepower handy to pull that off. Even this reinforced monster bitch of a door.

Afia rose to her feet as the others hyped themselves up. She was the smallest person here, so she could peek in and see things first. Javier and Sykora were going to rely on her the most going forward, especially if he was going to be busy keeping Sykora from getting out of hand.

That woman just might, yet.

The lethal, gray fishbowl hovered about three meters up, just below the door jamb, but high enough to not be in anybody's way if the dragoon needed to fire.

Javier was on the other side of the door, so Afia was able to peek as the door moved to one side. It opened sideways away from her side of the frame on slightly grinding rails, probably a bit of gunk in there somewhere from being closed too long. Common problem. One of the reasons you opened every door regularly as part of maintenance.

Inside was a vast chamber that took her breath away.

She gasped, but the others would see it soon enough, so she didn't need to say anything.

At least there was nothing to shoot.

The hatch slid the whole way open and disappeared into the bulkhead with a small thunk.

The air coming out had a different smell. Afia couldn't say what it was, but it was there.

The bridge of the *Neu Berne* Flagship *Hammerfield*.

Huge. Wasteful. Impressive.

From her vantage, it was a round room, about twenty-five meters across, with a domed ceiling at least nine meters at the peak.

Two meters in, stairs went down a meter to a walkway on either side of the four meter entryway.

Afia could see a number of crew stations around the outside of the bridge, but the central section was the most impressive.

Six stations arranged in a hexagon pattern, looking outward over the stations around the outer ring that faced the bulkhead.

It was the center that caught her eye and her breath.

A raised dais. A round pedestal maybe a meter tall and three across, with steps ringing it all the way around. A command station, similar to what the captain had, back on *Storm Gauntlet*, but bigger, more ornate.

And occupied.

A man sat there, facing them, unmoving.

Sykora had both guns out so fast that they might have always been there.

From her close proximity, Afia could see them shake, just the slightest bit.

About what Afia would have done, after a night of watching really good zombie movies.

The probe pinged the room hard. Afia felt it in her bones, the pulse was so heavy across so many frequencies. But it held its fire, so Afia assumed everything was good enough, at least for now.

"Sykora," Javier barked sharply.

Afia tore her eyes away from the bridge to look at her companions.

Javier was poised, his attention riveted on the dragoon, but he was carefully not interposing himself between Sykora and whatever terrible visions she was having. Sykora was an alabaster statue, except for the vibrating barrels, that image being possibly the most frightening thing Afia had ever seen in her life.

Djamila Sykora was normally the rock that the rest of the crew was built upon.

What would they do if she came apart on them?

Hajna and Sascha had peeked, but they had their fire lanes to maintain. Stone professionals.

That left Afia.

Internally, she shrugged.

You are an engineer. Treat this like an engineering problem.

Understand that sometimes, you have to go into a hostile reactor and die killing it for the good of the crew.

"Cover me," she said, stepping quickly forward and out of any lunging reach.

"Damn it, Afia," Javier said, but that was all.

She was pretty sure Sykora was keeping all of his attention.

The fans were on in here, a nice, background hum that meant *safe* on board a starship. Lights as well.

Heat. That was what was different.

The hallway had been four degrees, just enough above freezing that pipes with water weren't at risk. It was closer to eighteen degrees in here. Not quite warm enough to strip naked and enjoy the feel of nothing but breeze against her skin, but close.

Oh, so damned close.

The rest of the crew would probably still be in jackets and pants, but they hadn't grown up with a glacier across the valley, either.

Why would this room be so warm?

None of the other stations were inhabited, just the captain's. Afia paused after about four meters to slowly pivot in place and take it all in. Twelve stations along the outer wall. Six stations around the captain. And the throne.

From here, Afia could see a panel on the far wall, six meters by three, that roughly mirrored the entryway. Visual screen, but only for the captain, since everyone else was facing the wrong way usually.

Impressive as hell.

Afia took a deep breath. Her suit was reacting to the greater warmth by shutting down the heating elements. She wasn't suddenly chilled with fear, no, sir.

That's what she told herself.

She was an engineer. He was not a zombie, that unmoving man up there. Screw that.

She took another step closer, just to prove her own courage.

Okay, he's dead.

Dried up. Shriveled like a hunk of beef jerky.

Hard to tell how old he was, but Afia guessed him to be the actual captain. The red uniform he wore had enough bangles to be a senior officer of some sort.

Blond hair looked like it wanted to be graying, but hadn't quite made up its mind, yet.

Anglo, obviously. He had that pinkish tone to his skin that differentiated *Neu Berne* from her own Indonesian ancestors, even if she had grown up with her family in the Yukon Protectorate, back on Earth.

His head was tilted down, but she was short and he was on a riser, so Afia could see his face.

At least his eyes were closed.

She took another step closer.

He was fully strapped in, with his hands resting on the armrests, looking utterly peaceful.

There was a large, white envelope in his lap, but there was no way in hell she was getting that close.

"*Hammerfield*, please provide operational status," she called out to the room.

It had ignored Javier outside. Maybe it was deaf. Maybe it was asleep.

Maybe the bridge defensive systems were about to come live and try to kill her.

Afia had her doubts about that, as keyed up as the probe and the dragoon were, right now.

Nothing.

No change to the air systems blowing. No lights coming on or going off where she could see them.

"Afia?" Javier's voice carried across the vast distance that separated them right now.

She spun slowly in place again, taking it all in while she was still the first conqueror to set foot on this bridge.

"All clear," she said.

"Everyone in," she heard him order.

"No," Sykora said weakly. "We should not all be trapped in there."

"Djamila, we're going to stay together," Javier replied in a voice that he might use on a skittish horse.

Afia turned so she could watch the corpse and her friends at the same time.

Had they really found the last flagship and her crew?

BOOK NINETEEN: HAMMERFIELD

PART ONE

With both Djamila and Javier outside the ship, Zakhar was pulling a watch duty on the bridge, when he would normally leave it to the rest of his Centurions and their assistants and go do paperwork himself. He probably still should, but it was better if everyone else got some down time.

Lir himself only knew when something would happen, or what it would look like. This system was so messy, so complicated with gravity wells, that there really wasn't any safe way to trigger a jump longways across the entire system, punching home a goal between the primary star and the binary pair that had been captured later.

There was barely enough space to get a running start away from the ancient warship if it decided to come after them.

Zakhar hoped there was enough space.

Storm Gauntlet was old, but still dated to the period after the Great Wars had ended. She should be more advanced, technologically, than *Hammerfield*, even if the little corvette had been massively outgunned by the galleon before she had taken so much damage escaping *Svalbard*.

If *Neu Berne* had been more advanced, they wouldn't have lost so badly, taking down the *Union of Man*, *Balustrade*, and everyone but the *Concord*, quietly sitting over in one corner of the galaxy away from the main players.

Djamila and her team had gone silent as soon as they emerged from the flight bay. Zakhar had watched them cross the space on passive optics only, until they vanished from sight into the maw of the gray beast.

Javier made a pretty good Jonah, on reflection. Zakhar pondered, but was unable to identify where Nineveh might be, in the modern context. Or maybe, who?

"Clock time?" Zakhar called out.

Not because he couldn't look it up himself, but to remind everyone to stay sharp.

Tobias Gibney was manning the science station this shift. Thomas Obasanjo had gunnery. Mikhail Dominguez sat in the pilot's chair.

It was a tossup who would respond first. They were all pretty good, or they wouldn't be sitting on his bridge in a potentially dangerous situation.

"Ninety-four minutes since they boarded, sir," Gibney replied.

Zakhar wondered at what point he would have to decide to go rescue them, *rescue her*, or give up and get on with a post-piracy life, if no signal ever came.

No answer availed itself.

He keyed a comm channel.

"Wardroom," he said in as light a voice as he could fake right now. "Captain would appreciate some tea, please."

"Coming up," a man's voice replied.

Zakhar settled himself for a long night, wondering if he would ever see Djamila again.

And if not, when would Prince Charming surrender his dreams of happily-ever-after?

PART TWO

Javier watched the Amazon like his life depended on it. Even more than usual.

Sykora was wound like the strings on a violin right now, just waiting for some musical lunatic to come along and make her scream in agony.

She stared back at him with eyes that didn't have any iris, any color, at all.

Just black portals to hell.

"We'll do this together, Djamila," he said quietly. "This is a tomb, a war memorial, and will be treated as such. But I need you focused. The rest of the women can handle anything that comes along. Can you do this?"

He had seen this iron woman raging. Cunning. Embarrassed. Befuddled. Even drunk once, and singing martial folks songs in German.

He had never seen her on the edge of cracking up.

At least he would die quickly when she did, since Javier had no doubt he would be first on her shit list when she lost control and opened fire.

Sykora took a breath.

It was shallow, but indicated that she was listening. Hopefully unwinding and not unraveling.

She nodded, just as shallowly.

Nothing more, but enough to tell him she was in control, however fragile that hold was.

He would ask what the hell had come over the bronzed berserker, but he already knew. Or could hazard a guess.

That might be King Arthur himself, seated on that dais over there. This might be Avalon.

And it might also be Niflheim.

She hadn't shot him, yet, so Javier took a gamble and stepped into the room, trusting the pathfinders to cover the hallway and Suvi to shoot Sykora if push really came to shove.

Hopefully, Suvi understood how utterly weird things had gotten and wouldn't overreact.

Which was the strangest thing Javier could think of, on an already bizarre day.

He needed Sykora, galling as that thought was.

Eight steps in, Afia watched with the sort of feigned nonchalance that didn't fool anyone, but he let it slide.

"What have you got, kid?" he said to try to smooth over the general awkwardness.

A glance back revealed that Suvi had come into the room and side-slipped to one side so she could cover all the organics, living or dead, in a single arc of fire. Which said a lot about her read on things.

Sykora followed, like a marionette whose strings have tangled, lurching step by step when she was normally smooth grace itself. Javier figured she had recovered somewhat when she holstered both pistols and looked around, awe scribed on her face like a ten-year-old at a theme park.

"He's dead," Afia replied, pointing at the guy in the captain's chair. "Apparently left a note for you."

"Me?" Javier asked.

"I'm not grabbing it," she said, feet rooted firmly to the deck. "*Sentience* isn't responding, but it isn't shooting, either. What do you think, boss?"

Javier looked around quickly. Nothing amiss in here. Sascha had entered. Hajna was following, walking sideways like a crab.

"Afia," Sascha called. "What button closes the door?"

"[Enter] key," the tiny engineer yelled back. "Bottom left."

Sascha keyed it in, and Javier watched the door slide shut with a soft click.

Here they were.

Sykora had drifted closest to the corpse, but stayed at the bottom of the steps, like a peasant waiting her turn to present a petition.

No guns, and a minimum of fidgeting. Probably a good sign.

Javier walked noisily up to stand next to the giant woman. He could probably have tried to sneak and she'd have still tracked him, as keyed up as she appeared.

One glance over and he confirmed that there was still no green in those eyes.

Just white and black.

At least she wasn't as pale as she had been.

Javier sniffed, aware of what old corpses in space tended to smell like. It wasn't like the old, dried leather you got in the desert.

More stale and musty. Three-day-old bread, maybe.

"Probe," he said in a normal voice. "Status, please."

"All scans nominal," Suvi said in the dumb, computer voice she was hiding behind.

Again, she would warn him, hopefully. But there was an even bigger *Sentience* here. Maybe older. Maybe her age. A dangerous sibling, in any case.

Javier didn't think the dragon could sneak up and take Suvi over without a sound, or a fight.

But he really hadn't studied the Great War more than enough to ace his history exams at the Academy. And that was a long time ago.

Afia was twitchy. Sykora right out on the ledge. The pathfinders were trying to look every direction for zombies coming out of the vents and side doors.

That left him.

But this was why he got out of bed this morning.

Javier took a loud breath, deep and meaningful, as a warning to everyone else.

Not like what came next would be a surprise to anyone, but still.

He climbed the four steps to the platform, where he could stand next to the dead guy.

Uniform didn't mean anything either, except that the guy looked more like a captain and less like an admiral. Those people always had to get extra silly with their decorations.

Scarlet, long sleeve shirt. Not cotton, but something stretchy if still a little loose, with refractive elements in it that looked like glitter.

Glossy black, leather, slip-on boots to mid-calf. Black pants that were tight down through the thigh, and then flared out into little bells before tucking into the boots, like big, black mushrooms.

It was hard to tell the man's age, given that he was all dried up and wrinkly, but Javier would have guessed him around fifty when he died.

The face was calm in death. The arms relaxed on the armrests of his grand throne, like a king of yore.

He was composed.

At peace.

This man hadn't died in agony or horror. His corpse wasn't here as a warning to future generations or a trophy.

Javier looked down at the envelope in the man's lap. The paper was a cream color, almost almond. It was oversized, like a standard piece of paper folded in half, instead of thirds.

There was writing on the outside. Big, blocky letters.

This did not look like a man with a florid, cursive hand.

And he had placed it facing outward, so that it would be immediately legible to someone standing where Javier was, and upside down to the captain on his chair.

Javier picked it up and held the document in one hand, weighing it.

Heavy linen stock. Filled with several pages of the same weight inside, from the bulkiness.

Javier's German was pretty good, better spoken than written, but still competent enough if something was a scientific article. Less so with literature.

He was probably safe with this man.

"What does this say?" he turned to show it to the only native in the room. In the crew. Maybe it would help.

Djamila's eyes focused. Squinted a little. Her head came forward unconsciously, just a touch, but enough to break the fragile rigidity she had assumed.

She blinked.

Javier could see tears forming in her eyes. Happily, nobody else was in a position to perceive that. Something else he had never expected to know about this woman.

Possibly something else to carry to his grave.

Javier honestly hadn't believed that sort of thing was possible with Djamila Sykora.

But this was the future, and all things were possible.

"*We did our duty*," she said in a voice that managed both quiet reverence and that sort of profound heaviness that only *Neu Berne* culture ever conveyed.

"Yeah," Javier said. "That's what I thought."

Javier had a pretty good speaking voice, even translating something as he went, and he knew they would want to hear it.

He flipped it over, carefully peeled away the wax seal he found, and pulled out the pages folded up inside.

PART THREE

"ADMIRAL STEINER IS DEAD. She was the Last Admiral of Neu Berne, *as we measure such things, and the first casualty when the Intelligence went insane.*

That coward is dead now, and the survivors are trapped here. The technical crew who could have rebuilt things died with it, leaving the poor, sad remains of the crew locked inside our own mausoleum, like an ancient king who buries his household with him for the afterlife.

Hopefully, I will find a way to haunt that beast in hell.

To you who have found us here: Greetings.

The rogue Intelligence was destroyed, and with it most of our records, since we had no other way to read them. With nothing else to do, we repaired as much of the physical structure of the vessel as we could and parked this craft in the most constant orbit we could manage, a gravitationally-stable point where it would hopefully become a suitable monument.

Without the stardrives controlled by the Intelligence, or the main computer system that was its brain and memory, we could never leave this system, except to aim the vessel across the interstellar darkness at sub-light speeds, to become someone else's navigational hazard, several centuries after we had all died.

Our mission had been to escape Neu Berne. *To rally the outer colonies and worlds. To hide in the wilderness, like a young prince, and to reclaim the throne when he came of age.*

We have failed. And failed the Empire as well. We discussed allowing the knowledge of our failure to die with us, by flying into one of the three stars here, but in the end decided that we owed the future the truth of what had happened here.

I have left a written log in my cabin, begun after we had slain the beast and known our own death. The other logs were contained within the memory of the Intelligence, and so hidden from us.

Each death was recorded. Crew who succumbed to wounds from the final battle. Accidents as we rebuilt the ship to the finest standards possible before powering everything down for the longest night.

Finally, the day when there was no more we could do.

The crew retired to the main gymnasium, where we had an evening of the finest food and companionship, telling old stories, singing patriotic songs, and establishing the final bonds of comrades facing the eternal darkness.

The Medical Officer had prepared the potion. One by one the crew drank it and made their final peace with God.

Each man and woman retired to the coffins that were their final resting place, bid their comrades Auf Wiedersehen, *and closed the lids, to sleep the eternal and find their place to Valhalla.*

Only I remained, a captain dying with his ship. It was my duty to record it all, return to my bridge, and await you.

I am Captain Ulrich Mayer, last commander of the last flagship of the Neu Berne *Navy.*

I failed my Empire, but I have done my duty.

PART FOUR

Javier took a breath and looked up.

Sykora was crying openly now. But that was okay. So were the other three women. Probably the fourth as well.

She was human in all the ways that mattered.

Everyone who traveled in space had to face that risk. Dying, alone in the darkness, trapped farther away from friends and home than you can ever return.

Lost, and never coming home.

Javier nodded to Captain Mayer, a very short, formal thank you for everything the man had done for a future generation in need.

It made sense now. The *Sentience* hadn't responded to him or Afia because it was dead.

He wondered how much they had been able to repair.

Most people thought of a *Sentience* as a giant computer program, billions of lines of code capable of responding to ever more complicated decisions trees.

Javier knew better.

At her core, Suvi was a very compact set of algorithms embedded on a set of chips. Not ROM, the read-only-memory that is etched into the board and never modified again, but a firmware that was non-volatile and could be improved over time by someone who took the time to understand how the language worked at that level.

To help her be more human.

If he was only ever going to know one daughter, to make sure she turned out a pretty good kid.

Suvi had.

It was her memories that took up all the damned space, even written in the multi-dimensional symbolic language that her kind used to encode everything. Cleaning up systems she had been using must have been what it was like to have teenagers in the house.

Hopefully, the captain had killed the beast by pulling or destroying the chips at the core of the system, and not just blowing up the central computer itself.

"So now what?" Afia breathed in a quiet voice, as if unwilling to break the tableau that had formed around them like icicles.

Javier studied Sykora's face for a clue. That woman did not understand poker one damned bit, wearing her emotions on her sleeves most of the time.

Today, she had either gone deeper inside herself than he had ever seen, or peeled away all the layers that had accumulated like an angry pearl over the years, to show the grain of stone at the center of it all.

Six months ago, he would have happily used everything he was learning to drive this woman bat-shit insane. More bat-shit insane.

But that was yesterday. And this was tomorrow.

"Djamila?" he said simply.

Her eyes came back from the horizon, flickered over to his face.

Bright green emeralds, lit with an internal flame.

"Now we know," she murmured.

Javier nodded. One of the galaxy's greatest mysteries in the last century, and they had solved it.

The little evil conscience on his left shoulder showed him a bill of goods they could sell to the happy folks at *Neu Berne* when they returned the last crew to their homeland.

Ransom, if you will.

The planet was poor these days, but even a poor planetary government worked with sums that make interstellar corporations look like popsicle stands by comparison.

Not that he would ever breathe a word of this to Sykora.

The good conscience on his right shoulder walked over and knocked the evil one onto his ass with a roundhouse, just like in the cartoons.

He turned back to Afia, patiently waiting by his side as the emotional tides swirled around her and started to head back out to sea.

"Now, we go look at the engineering sections and see how much work it will take to get everything in motion," he said.

"What about *Storm Gauntlet*?" she asked carefully. "Should we call the captain?"

All of the women were suddenly staring intently at him. But that was okay.

He had been planning this for a long time.

"Soon," he said. "It will be much easier to use the ship's comm to send a signal, as noisy as this system is."

Javier pointed at the dead man that had come to dinner.

"And we only have his word that they didn't set a trap for us," Javier continued. "Let's not suck the whole crew into an ambush."

Sykora came back to herself. Feisty. Tough.

Intent.

But she held her peace, for now.

That would make it easier.

Afia turned to the dragoon.

"Best way into engineering?" she asked the tall woman.

"Deck Thirteen," Sykora said. "Elevators should be working, but let's take the central stairs anyway."

Javier nodded. As long as Sykora remained tactical, everything would be fine.

Zakhar Sokolov was probably the only one of them sneaky enough to anticipate what was coming.

PART FIVE

AFIA WAS ALMOST at the back of the column. The group of them was approaching the port staircase element that ran vertically down the center of the ship, walking along the port-side hallway that served as one of the three boulevards from bow to stern on Deck Four.

Everything had a chilled smell, kinda like you got in a brand new refrigerator, before any food had managed to leave an impression.

Metal and plastic and cold.

It was weird on a starship, not to smell people and leftover dinners.

She had let everyone else organize themselves as they tromped noisily through the intestines of the big ship. And it was big.

If you could have opened up the right frames and access points, the combined cargo deck down the ship's axis was almost big enough to carry *Storm Gauntlet*, a fierce, little teacup Chihuahua in a lady's purse.

Not that Afia had ever been compared that way either. Especially not as tiny as she was compared to most folks. Being small, and fierce, and technical, she had stood out from the other kids.

Afia Burakgazi had grown up on Earth, almost exactly half a world away from her family's ancestral homeland of Indonesia where all her cousins still lived. In the Yukon Protectorate there were still wild places and dangerous critters. You had to keep an eye and an ear tuned to things out of the ordinary and be prepared to listen when your subconscious is trying to tell you something.

Plus, her grandmother was a witch, and had hexed her early on with the Second Sight.

Both her nose for trouble and her grandmother's memory were talking to her now.

The dragoon was an emotional wreck. No ifs, ands, or buts about it.

Afia probably would be, too, in similar circumstances.

But all of the snark and bickering had disappeared from Javier.

Gone.

Like frost in the morning sun.

He was treating Sykora carefully. Kid gloves.

If there was ever a time to score points on her, it was now, when she was in no shape to fight back.

Afia probably would have had to get up in his face, if he had. Sascha and Hajna as well. But he would have said something.

It was the nature of the relationship between those two.

Except he hadn't. Hadn't even come close.

Nothing.

He had to be up to something.

Afia didn't think that anybody but her had picked it up, or someone would have said something. And maybe she was only imagining it, but she didn't think so. Javier Aritza, occasionally infamous as Eutrupio Navarre, was hands-down the sneakiest man Afia had ever met.

So she watched the way he moved, one place ahead of her in line and a head taller. He didn't walk enough steps every day for the suit to look good on his ass.

They arrived.

The central stairs were a strange design.

The designer here had done something weird. And not just because this was a cargo ship with a big empty space down the middle.

There were two sets of stairs here: Port side and Starboard, well away from the central boulevard. Sascha had picked port for no better reason than she could. The two were identical.

On most ships, a stairwell ran top to bottom in an open column, with emergency plates that could close horizontally between levels if you lost power and pressure. Plus, they had hatches out at every floor that were normally closed.

Here, it was a set of tall rooms.

You went down a level and the stairs ended. You had to go through a hatch at the bottom of the stairs and into another chamber, turn one-hundred-eighty degrees, and go down another flight in another room.

Each pair of levels was sealed automatically, plus you got a lot more structural strength at the center of the ship because you didn't have that big, vertical column.

But it was a serious pain in the ass to go down nine decks this way.

Afia wondered if that was part of the reason Sascha had done it. Maybe she hoped the grumbling would get Sykora back to being herself.

Afia considered that maybe she needed to walk more steps every day, too, when they got down to Deck Thirteen.

Her legs felt like rubber, her butt hurt, and she was short of breath.

Sykora looked like she had just come from the beach. Hajna and Sascha, too.

Afia kept her grumbles to herself.

Mostly.

At one point, the probe pivoted around enough that she was looking at its "face," so maybe the grumbles weren't that quiet.

Afia worked on keeping her mouth shut after that.

Thanks, Mom.

Deck Thirteen looked a lot like Deck Four if you didn't

paint it as often. Not dingy or anything, but faded a bit, maybe. Monochrome. No little trim flashes or color offsets to brighten things.

Soulless.

The land of the introverts who went into the engineering tracks, rather than the extroverts who did the line command or ground combat tracks.

Out the last stairwell door and along this hallway to the aft. The cargo holds were down here, and huge in places. Several decks tall and a hundred meters between frames. Big enough for a hockey rink, stands, and a taco truck.

Engineering, when they got there, wasn't nearly as impressive, but Afia wasn't sure what she had been expecting.

Sure, big machines everywhere. Control room with transparent windows on this level, so you could watch several parallel rows of monstrous power reactors lined up like ugly, gray turtles on a log.

But nothing she hadn't seen recently on *Storm Gauntlet*, or before she became a pirate.

The room smelled like a power station, too. Lubricant and ozone in trace amounts. The faintest hint of rust and metal, like tiny shavings spalled off by slowly moving parts.

It felt good to be home.

She dropped automatically into the primary station, wiped the screen clean of accumulated *stuffff* with a rag she kept handy for just that task, and powered it up. These was dust everywhere, but nothing bad. Trust a *Neu Berne* crew, especially with nothing better to do before they died, to clean everything as well as humanly possible.

At least the folks had unlocked everything before they died, so that someone like her could put this old beast back into the line.

"What's your pleasure?" she smiled up at Javier.

He looked down at her for a second, blank, before a roguish smile ghosted itself and he winked back at her. More of a promise, since this was probably not the time nor the place.

Probably.

You never knew.

"Make sure everything is intact on standby and no more than a soft yellow," he said. "If we think the life support systems are solid, start bringing things up to the same temperature as the bridge was. That should be good enough for now. All the food that's left is long past edible, so I'm not worried about it, but I don't want it so warm that cans explode."

"Coming up," she said, starting to toggle through screens.

Things being written in German on this ship didn't bother her. Everything down here would be written in *Engineer*, a standard thousands of years old that spanned all forms of communication.

She could identify the workarounds the crew had programmed into the systems when the *Sentience* died. It would mostly handle those tasks for everyone, needing only occasional tuning and maintenance to keep it all working.

A vessel this big probably kept a smaller crew than a little corvette like *Storm Gauntlet* had.

Afia didn't trust the life support systems all that much, but they had held under a low baseline load for a very long time, so she was comfortable telling them to bring the temperature and pressure up slowly.

Everyone would remain in their suits until she said otherwise. That point, she would hammer home on all of them.

Fierce teacup Chihuahua.

"Can you access comm systems from in here?" Javier asked in a voice that just sounded wrong.

Concerned, but evasive. Like he really wanted the answer to be no, but couldn't just come out and say that, at least not in front of the others.

Weird.

But this was Javier, and he was having to juggle everything else with Sykora being possessed by demons or something. Maybe it was just the struggle to keep them all sane that was getting to him.

Afia toggled through a couple of boards and ran through logic trees while he watched. The other three just waited, torn between watching the big generators and paying attention to what she was doing.

She could take advantage of their paranoia to help Javier.

They didn't need to know that someone had defaulted all login accounts to Full System Administrator rights. And she would fix that pretty soon. That was too much like handing a five-year-old a beam weapon. Stupid, and someone was going to get hurt.

"I can transmit a signal on the right frequencies as part of the Identification Transponder," Afia shaded the truth with a small forest of pine trees. "Is that good enough?"

That must have been the answer to his prayers. Javier sagged just a little, and smiled at her.

"Perfect," he replied. "Let *Storm Gauntlet* know we have boarded, are exploring, and are safe at present. We will check in again in ten hours."

"Ten?" Sykora perked up from her fugue with a voice that was a thin ghost of her normal bark, but you could still hear the woman underneath.

"That's right," Javier pivoted to look up at her. "We've had a long day, a lot of stress, and the ship needs time to come up from her nap. This is a good time to eat, sleep, and when we wake up, we can probably get out of these damned suits and live like normal people."

"Watch cycle?" Sascha chimed in, obviously intent on handling things if her boss was off-line.

"None," Javier said, his voice gone hard and flat, like a sword blade. "The probe can handle everything. I want you all down hard and fully refreshed tomorrow. Take something if you need to. There are a whole bunch of dead men and women on this ship and we will need to secure them with the proper ceremonies. Everything else that comes after that will be even more difficult. Questions?"

The three women subsided.

Afia nodded, but only inside her head. Javier *was* up to something.

That was a sneaky way to ambush somebody.

Afia called up a schematic to check the location.

"There is a break room behind that door," she said, pointing through the transparent wall to a space down a little ways, right next to the first power generator on the starboard side. "It should have bunks. I'll sleep here so I can be ready if the system sounds any alerts."

Javier didn't look too thrilled with that option, but he couldn't argue with her.

Kinda like how he had boxed the others in.

And, while she was thinking about it, Afia reached into the console in the break room and locked out certain functions.

If Javier was up to something, she might need to help. Or she might also have to shoot him.

PART SIX

JAVIER WAS FIRST into the big area Afia had classified as a break room. Twenty meters long, by about half that wide, it looked like a wardroom, with all the tables and chairs around the open space and locked down for loss of gravity. Ugly gray walls and ceiling. Moss green carpet in the kind of mottled pattern that would hide stains and spills.

There was a wall of vending machines on the far wall from him, plus a couple of coffee robots. Every single one was dark and empty.

Trust people who thought like Sykora to clean out the machines of all the chips and candy. They had probably drained the water lines on the coffee makers as well.

He would appreciate that in a few days, after someone like Ilan Yu had spent a great deal of time cleaning it all down and replacing parts, but right now a little caffeine could be nice. Sleep was the last thing on his mind.

The right end of the room was a bunch of cubicle doors. Every ship he had ever served on had something similar in their engineering bays. People might be on duty for long stretches, but they got frequent breaks, and needed to study for certifications and such.

Much better if all your engineers were immediately available in any emergency down here.

"Probe. Access Command Mode," he called, loud enough for the three women coming through the door behind him. Suvi was already listening. "Secure this room for engineering emergencies and remain on watch here."

"Confirmed," Suvi replied in her bored computer voice.

Javier took one last look and turned to face Sykora. He was exhausted, but was going to push right through. He let the exhaustion color his voice, though.

"You should take something, or meditate yourself to sleep," he said before looking at the two other women. "I plan to be asleep in about five minutes. Set your alarms for eight hours and be prepared to go like hell for sixteen hours tomorrow."

He didn't bother waiting for them to answer. Instead, he went into the closest cubicle and closed the door.

Locked it, too, just in case either Hajna or Sascha decided that they needed his help to be knocked off-line for a while.

Any other day than this…

The space beyond the door was cozy. Two meters wide by four deep. Single bunk with a thin blanket. Writing desk surface with a chair. Softer paint on the walls, here a soothing rose color.

He pulled the control remote for the probe from his pack and settled himself on the bed. A switch and the voice channel was active.

"You ready?" he asked.

The walls were also going to be totally sound-proof, because someone napping or studying didn't need to listen to someone else snoring.

"All set here," Suvi replied in her usual bright voice. "How long?"

Javier considered his options.

"Let's give them an hour to settle and get into deep sleep," Javier said. "Wake me then. Afia will need time, as well."

"Got it, boss," his sidekick chirped.

Javier laid down and closed his eyes.

AFIA WATCHED them on a security camera in the break room and let go a deep breath. She listened in as Javier went off to bed first, the other three taking only a few moments to decide to do the same, the general consensus that the probe would be enough watch for now.

And it had been a long day. Up for hours before the long flight over here. All the stress of deep space with a hostile warship looming. Breaking and entering into a tomb.

Afia was as exhausted as Javier sounded.

Still, something just wasn't right, but she couldn't put her finger on it.

Given her supreme control of the engineering boards, Afia temporized. She could nap, after setting alarms that would go off in her control room if anyone opened the door to the break area. It could even be loud, since this room was sealed up tight right now.

Anyone who came out in less than seven hours would be up to no good, anyway, so she needed to be able to block them from doing something stupid.

That done, Afia locked every door around her, stretched out on the floor, and let the strain of the day draw her down into darkness.

Beep.

Afia came awake instantly, lost for a second as an unfamiliar gray ceiling loomed overhead.

Engineering Primary Control. Door alarm. *Hammerfield.*

Afia was on her side on the deck, facing the control station. The screen was on, set to beep every three seconds until she disabled it. She studied movement on the camera's view.

Beep.

Javier had opened the door to the break room and come out into the main engineering space next to Auxiliary Power Unit number 1.

The probe, that armed eyeball with all the good sensors, was with him, so Afia lay still. If he went anywhere else, she would have to track him, and that might be hard.

Necessary, but hard.

What the hell would he need to be up to on this ship by himself?

She remained like a cold stone, just in case, but Javier quickly crossed to the main hatch outside her office, only glancing over once to make sure she was still asleep.

Afia had planned this, with enough of her back to the window to look like she was asleep, but she could see a screen he couldn't, not from outside.

And then he was out in the hallway.

She gave him a two count as the board continued to beep.

Afia was about to get up and move when the door alarm went off a second time, out of sequence.

On the screen, Sascha had also just opened the door and emerged.

Javier had looked ever so slightly furtive, walking almost hunched over and hurried. Sascha looked pissed. Like she had the same idea about Javier as Afia had, but wasn't necessarily planning to be as friendly. Certainly, the two of them weren't going off to fool around somewhere, since they could have done that in the break cubicles.

No, she was trailing him, and doing it secretly.

Which made sense. Sascha and Hajna were Sykora's people. Her hand-picked ground experts.

Apparently, Sascha had picked up on something and waited, just as Afia had.

Afia waited for the pathfinder to disappear out the door as well. Sascha didn't even bother to glance in at Afia, and then she was out in the corridor.

Afia counted to five, but she remained alone.

She climbed to her feet and disabled all the alarms. If those two were off to cause trouble, she needed to be after them quickly. If Sykora or Hajna came out, hopefully they would stay put for everyone else to come back here.

Assuming everyone was still alive.

Afia checked the pistol on her hip and made sure it was set to stun.

Always better to shoot first if things got ugly, but even better if you could make a mistake and correct it later.

THE HALLWAY JAVIER and Sascha had taken was rather dim.

Afia had programmed the thermostat to bring things shipwide up to eighteen degrees, but that would take about twelve hours to complete. In the meantime, she had left all the lighting down at the default levels. There was no reason to drop a sudden load on generators she hadn't personally inspected and certified.

The door was silent to open, letting Afia slip out and peek around the corner. This corridor ran transverse, starboard to port.

Nobody starboard.

She turned and looked port, trying to keep as silent as possible.

Movement of a shadow caught her eye. Afia leaned out a little farther with the patience of spring thaw.

Sascha, headed away from her. Peeking around another corner down the way, kinda like Afia was, so hopefully the other woman was tracking Javier and he was apparently headed aft.

Afia looked down and realized that she was going to make noise, walking in her boots on a metal floorway, no matter how stealthy she tried. Sascha was trained for these sorts of things. Probably Javier as well.

For a moment, she considered her options.

She was naked under the suit except for a t-shirt.

That was standard in an EVA. You had things to plug in to handle all your bio functions in space.

Sascha was still wearing her suit. Javier had been as well.

Most people would probably consider even eighteen degrees too damned cold to be out without a jacket on, to say nothing of pants or shoes. Right now, the ship was mostly five or maybe seven degrees above freezing.

Growing up in the Yukon Protectorate had taught her to be tough, walking without shoes as soon as it was warm enough. She'd never tried it *sans* pants.

Sascha disappeared around the corner, a gray ghost chasing another ghost.

Oh, well.

Afia holstered her pistol and ran her hands down the central seam in front to split the suit open. It was a soft suit inside the ship, without pressure. It was designed to turn more rigid in space when a tear on a sharp corner could be lethal.

Pop the crown upwards. Disconnect the neck collar. Grab the right glove and pull. Slip the arm free. Get the left arm loose. Get your shoulders clear of the suit. Drop on your butt and use the slack to reach inside and disconnect the plumbing. Must suck for boys. Girls just had a cup with a vacuum seal. Wriggle out of the boots and leggings.

Afia stood up in nothing but an old blue t-shirt she had gotten from the purser so long ago that she forgot where he had bought it.

The air circulation felt good on her legs. Goose pimples.

Almost like home.

She bent down, grabbed the pistol out of the holster, and padded after the pathfinder like she was stalking a deer.

Down to the corner. Kneel on stubby legs to get very, very low. Peek slowly, since motion drew the eye.

There.

Sascha was just approaching the hatch to the primary aft stairwell. Afia leaned back until just an eye, and ear, and some hair were visible, and froze.

Sure enough, Sascha drew her pistol and opened the hatch. She turned once and looked back, but it was cursory. She wasn't expecting anyone behind her, just covering her bases in case Javier had doubled back or something.

The short brunette slipped through the hatch and let it close behind her.

Afia waited a three-count, and then was out in the hall, jogging down to where the other woman has disappeared. These doors were pretty quiet. Hopefully, Sascha had gone far enough up or down that she wouldn't hear it open behind her.

Afia cycled the hatch, pistol mostly out of sight behind her, in case someone was standing there.

Nothing.

Afia remembered to breathe. She stepped in and let the door close.

Something clomped from above her.

Afia walked right to the edge and looked up. There was a gap there, a vertical column of air no bigger than a sparrow, but enough that she could see a silent shadow just a deck above her, and a noisy one only two decks above that, both headed upwards.

Javier and the probe. Being stalked by the pathfinder with the angry face.

With a curious engineer at the tail of the chain. Or, at least she hoped she was the end of the sneaking line.

Afia wondered how silly it would look if all five of them ended up chasing after each other. She refused, however, to look behind her.

The clunking paused before it suddenly faded, and then disappeared.

If she was counting correctly, Javier had just exited on Deck Eight.

Afia felt an icicle run down her spine. The only thing remotely interesting on Deck Eight was the primary access chamber for the computer cores, most of the hardware and redundant systems residing there and on Deck Nine.

What the hell was Javier doing that he wanted to get at the dead *Sentience*'s systems with nobody else around?

Sascha sped up a moment later, thumping quickly up the stairs until she stopped, presumably at the hatch on Deck Eight.

Afia followed, but she was in nowhere near as good a shape as the other woman. Jogging suggested itself in her future, rather than just using the elliptical machines and low weights to meet Captain Sokolov's monthly fitness requirements for the crew.

Hopefully, she wouldn't come around a landing and run into the other woman.

Last flight.

Afia gasped as she drove her aching thighs down the home stretch, cold air competing with burning muscles to see who would win.

She was going to need a long, hot bath tomorrow, preferably with a cute towel boy running to get her rum-based tiki-drinks at a regular basis.

Top step.

There was nobody there. And no other sounds above her.

She doubled over and sucked air like a badly-tuned motor vehicle running on petroleum distillates instead of batteries. Sounded like one, too.

Breath mostly caught, she keyed the hatch and hoped for the best, a ten-year-old chasing will-o'-th'-wisps again.

Nothing in the hallway. That was good.

She was on an aft, port corner of this deck as she emerged. One hallway went forward. One went sideways.

She peeked around a corner from her knees again and saw

Sascha ducked into a doorway well forward. Javier was a shadow, headed away with the probe by his side.

For a moment, snippets of conversation echoed but the words were garbled. Javier talking, a woman answering.

Huh.

Afia waited until Sascha moved. The pathfinder was silent, but focused entirely forward.

Afia dashed quietly across the hall into the corridor that ran across the ship. She had a good notion where Javier was headed, just not why.

But if she crossed the hip bones of the ship, she could move quickly up the starboard hallway and hopefully get close to things when whatever *it* was happened.

Afia could tell from the way Sascha moved that the woman was not going to be a pleasant person.

Hopefully, Javier wasn't doing anything so remotely stupid that she had to help Sascha kill him.

"ARE you sure this is a good idea?" Suvi asked him.

Javier cocked on eye at his floating sidekick as he walked quietly forward down the long, gray hallway. The ship's fans had kicked up a notch, adding a soft buzz, but the air circulating up here was only slowly heating up.

The place had a feel like a desert. Midnight in the dead of winter, when things were bone dry and chilling cold that cut through you.

It even smelled like dead sand.

"This ship is mine under any interstellar law you want to research," Javier replied. "Salvage has always applied on any derelict after twenty years abandoned."

"I meant sneaking away from everybody in the dead of night," she said with a huff. "Rough way to start a business partnership."

"We aren't partners yet," he growled. "And Sykora's so close to the edge that I'm not sure what is going to trigger her into a homicidal rage. From there, we're one step to a killing spree and I'll be the first victim."

"I'm faster than she is," Suvi observed tartly.

"I need her alive," he said. "All of the pirates are going to have to die before I'm safe from them. That means Sykora watching my back. Doubly so after this."

"But you don't really trust her," Suvi said. "What about Sokolov?"

"When I'm negotiating from strength, we'll see," Javier said. "Remember, that man made slaves of both of us. He might have upgraded me to a centurion, but that was all fast talking on my part. You could be dead right now, or wiped clean and reprogrammed as a toaster."

She growled under her breath, which was what he had intended.

Sokolov was one of *them*. And Javier hadn't yet found the limits to the man's honesty and honor, but he suspected they would be pushing the envelope on this one.

"You just missed the hallway," Suvi commented in that dry, arch tone of superiority he occasionally hated himself for teaching her.

Javier stopped and turned back to his right. He had gotten so wrapped up talking to his friend that he had missed what he was doing.

But that was why he kept her around. To keep him on the mostly-straight and not-particularly-narrow path.

Yep. Walked right by it.

Javier went back three paces and turned into the side hallway. The idiot who had designed this ship had a thing for doors on the exact centerline of the ship, rather than entering big spaces from either side. It would have made the spine stronger, with fewer hallways running side to side, but every culture had its quirks.

Naval architecture just magnified the weirdness by several orders of magnitude and cast it permanently into steel and exotic alloys.

"Which door?" he said.

Suvi had already knocked his attention span a little sideways. Let her navigate for a bit.

Her flashlight came on and speared a door on the forward side of the hall.

Javier approached.

It was another one of those over-wrought portals, like up on the bridge.

These people couldn't just make a hatch.

No, access to the computer core's primary space required a *statement.*

Javier suspected that it was the sort of intellectual rigidity that had caused them to fail originally. The *Concord* was way looser about that sort of thing, relying on smart people without browbeating them into behaving.

Javier reached over and keyed the panel.

The door split down the middle and disappeared silently into the bulkheads on both sides.

Inside, the space was unimpressive as he entered, until he looked down.

Deck Eight was the mezzanine for a larger space down on Nine. The floor under his feet was an open grate, which let warm air rise and pool, making the atmosphere here pleasant.

Javier hadn't realized how cold his face had gotten until now.

There was just the faintest hint of ozone here as well. Lots of big, powerful processing nodes, holding bits and pieces, *shards,* of *Hammerfield's* memories and brains scattered all over the place, while keeping it all as close to the exact center of the ship as possible.

"Where?" he asked.

The probe flew a little to the right, tilted down, and pointed a light over the railing at a machine that dominated the space below, a squat ziggurat nearly two decks tall.

Javier turned to the left and located the stairwell down. The steps were all open grate sides and treads.

The place felt oppressive. The engineering bays had been bland, but that was because engineers tended to be boring people to begin with. They didn't go in for bright colors and cheery design aesthetics. Made them nervous.

This place seemed designed to impress upon the visitor how insignificant they were.

Which made a queer bit of sense, when you thought about it. The being that had lived there had been the flagship of an entire star culture made up of crazy warrior berserkers.

Death before dishonor.

Probably committed seppuku for the slightest embarrassment.

Sykora and her ilk were never the kind to wake up from a three-day bender in a different county, wearing someone else's pants and a stolen Shore Patrol helmet.

Weirdoes.

His boots squeaked on the treads. Just because, he held the safety railing.

Better safe than stupid at this late date.

Down on Deck Nine, the ziggurat was even more brutal to behold, like some ancient monument to a dark and demanding god.

Maybe it was.

The metal was matte black, instead of the boring gray of everything else. There was a display screen for the *Sentience*, and of course it was four meters tall instead of one.

Javier glanced around for bushes that might catch fire as a warning.

Finding none, he wandered around to the right side, the designer apparently having been right-handed, and drew a small socket gun from the tools on his belt. Javier already knew that *Neu Berne* used some weird, local variant of metric measurements for tools, so he had swapped everything out before he left *Storm Gauntlet*.

The panel he wanted was at shoulder level, and about a meter wide, by half that tall, held in place with six countersunk bolts. He started at the bottom left, seated the socket gun over it and pushed the thumb button on the back to grab the bolt head. A moment later, he pulled the trigger and the socket gun grabbed the bolt.

Trust *Neu Berne* to use a ten centimeter long, machine-threaded bolt to hold a simple metal panel in place.

Middle bottom next. Bottom right. Top right. Top left, until the panel was held in place by only the top center bolt.

Javier put his left hand on the panel to hold it in place and undid the last panel. He dropped all six bolts into a pouch and holstered the socket gun on his belt.

The panel dropped away to reveal a motherboard with twelve slots, all open.

"Light, please," he said, leaning forward.

Suvi put her spotlight into the space.

Huh. Standard design, right across the board.

Javier had always wondered how such a consciously-militant culture had handled their tech.

Apparently, they had outsourced to the good, little merchants of the *Concord* for parts.

Made sense. *The Concord* was the only relatively neutral nation in the entire quadrant big enough and sophisticated enough to handle something like that.

Sure, they had generally supported the *Union of Man*, but that was more from a standpoint of not letting *Neu Berne*'s mad dreams of galactic conquest come to fruition, rather than some ideological thing.

And it let the *Concord* sell gear profitably to both sides.

That helped, because this was suddenly going to be way easier than he had hoped.

Javier had feared he would have to rewire this entire section of the ship, unconsciously expecting those yahoos to have gone and invented something completely insane to run their ships.

He could work with this.

"You ready, kid?" he asked his sidekick.

"You have no idea how long I've been looking forward to this," she replied.

"Well, deploy your landing gear, put yourself down here, and pop your panels," he said. "You'll take a quick nap and wake up a whole new woman."

"Rawr," she purred.

The probe set down, opened itself like a steamer trunk, and went dark.

Javier reached in and popped the first chip-board loose.

Each was about the size of a deck of cards on a side, by about half that thick. In a moment, he had all eight out and arrayed on the deck in front of him, in the exact order he would put them into the ziggurat's brain.

The greatest act of piracy in a century.

Javier sighed a little as he picked up the first two boards. Never again would he have his dangerous sidekick running around down on a planet with him.

Radio lag was too great for her to control something from orbit, and she would be a starship for however many centuries after his death as she could maintain and upgrade herself.

But that was a problem for next week.

Javier rose and smiled.

A voice came out of nowhere, somewhere behind him.

A woman. A very angry woman.

"Don't you dare move, you son of a bitch."

PART NINE

Fortunately for Afia, her quarry was in no hurry to get anywhere, convinced he was the only one awake right now. And the dangerous probe was obviously distracted as well.

The dim corridors helped Afia, since she didn't cast much of a shadow as she jogged, first lateral and then fore. She even had time to catch her breath, ducked out of sight and listening to Javier talk to some woman who absolutely wasn't Sascha.

He hadn't managed to call for reinforcements from somewhere else, had he?

Not a chance.

But then, who was he talking to? The probe?

Afia had heard the probe's voice before. The one he had programmed to communicate verbally, and not just via the little portable remote he carried around. It sounded like that in tone, but this sounded like a real person talking, having a conversation with Javier.

He hadn't been able to program his survey remote to be that smart, had he? How much programming had he done on his old *Sentient* Probe-Cutter? Enough to make her sound like that?

This was Javier. He would absolutely program it to sound female. Not in a sexist way. No, just because he preferred women. Smart women.

Competent women.

She hadn't heard him mention anything about that significant of an upgrade, though, and the probe had been dumb and monotonous just a few hours ago.

If she sounded that smart now, then she had been then, as well. Which meant she had been hiding.

What would be so important that he had to hide her in a survey…?

Afia nearly screamed.

Ground her jaws. Clenched her fists.

Considered banging her head against the steel behind her, if there was any way to do it silently where Sascha wouldn't hear.

Javier hadn't programmed her to be that smart. That sassy.

Well, no, he probably had, but not in the last month.

Maybe ten years ago.

Javier had told the captain that the boards containing the cognition matrix for the *Sentience* back on his old ship had been destroyed. That Javier had killed her rather than letting the slavers have her.

Afia had been part of the crew that cut up the carcass later, so that Javier could salvage his arboretum and his chickens. After the woman who was Javier's pilot was dead.

Except she wasn't dead.

Somehow, he had rescued her, like an ancient princess in a fairy tale, and brought her here.

And he was about to enter *Hammerfield's* Primary Processing Core, where he could somehow transfer her into the gigantic warship, bringing her back to life with a kiss.

Afia wanted to scream.

Javier as Prince Charming.

Afia suddenly saw the gray sphere not as an eyeball, but an egg.

Holy crap!

Afia managed to not move. Not breathe.

Not scream.

In the hallway around the corner and behind her, Javier passed through the hatch into silence.

Afia peeked out to confirm.

She waited. Patience, itself.

Right on cue, Sascha appeared, one of the ancient, Greek Furies, goddesses of divine retribution, coming for Javier's soul.

What would she do when she discovered the truth?

More silence as the other woman opened the door and vanished within.

What the hell was Afia supposed to do now? Call the dragoon? Captain Sokolov?

How?

She had left all her electronics back with her pants. All she had now was her gun.

It would be up to her to decide what happened next. Sascha Koç would absolutely kill Javier. She knew that much.

Afia sucked down a hard, dry breath, past a tongue grown too big for her mouth.

She rose, absolutely covered in goose pimples for the first time today, and padded over to the door.

She hoped enough time had passed for Sascha to move away from the hatch before it opened.

The last thing she needed right now was a firefight.

Afia keyed the door and tried to look as innocent as she could manage, half-naked and armed.

Sascha wasn't there when it opened.

Afia stepped in and slid to her right, backing her bottom up against a cold, steel bulkhead as the hatch closed and she tried to find everyone.

The space was huge. Not quite as big as down in engineering. Way bigger than the bridge.

Two decks' worth of space, and she was looking down, between her big toes, at the steel grate that made up this level.

Nobody on this level. Which was good. This space was barely ten meters deep by thirty wide, with catwalk stairs down on her left.

Sascha was at the bottom of the staircase, crouched down and looking every direction except up.

From where she stood, above, Afia caught motion on the right side of a big, black, monument-thingee.

Javier. And the egg.

"You ready, kid?" Javier asked the air.

"You have no idea how long I've been looking forward to this," the woman's voice came back a second later.

There was no doubt in Afia's mind that she was hearing with a person, and not a stupid computer system. The warmth of the tones guaranteed that.

The longing.

"Well, deploy your landing gear, put yourself down here, and pop your panels," Javier said. "You'll take a quick nap and wake up a whole new woman."

"Rawr," the woman replied.

Afia nearly laughed. The egg sounded just about exactly how she had always envisioned Javier's perfect woman would. Probably tall and blond as well, though Javier had shown himself to be remarkably open to all shapes and sizes, for as long as she had known him.

Movement on her left caught Afia's eye.

Sascha creeping forward, oblivious to anything except the betrayal unfolding.

Javier had knelt and opened the sphere like a standing suitcase. He pulled a half-dozen boards from inside and put them on the deck in front of him, pausing for a moment as if in prayer.

Perhaps, asking for the woman's forgiveness? Or the gods of the cosmos itself, as he was about to unleash a powerful avenging angel.

And who would these two pursue? Had this all been a ruse to get here, so he could draw the captain in and kill *Storm Gauntlet*?

Javier owed them all a serious debt of pain.

Was he about to collect?

Javier picked up two boards and stood.

Sascha watched from the corner of the big device, a pistol in hand. Every line on the woman screamed rage at Javier's unfaithfulness.

The pistol came up, an extension of Sascha's fist.

"Don't you dare move, you son of a bitch," Sascha cried.

Javier spun about in surprise, eyes agog.

Literally, hand in the cookie jar.

Even from the shadows overhead, Afia could watch the anger slowly overtake the surprise in his face as the two stared hard at each other for long seconds.

Afia knew Javier had slept with Sascha. More than once. Enjoyed the same casual relationship with her that he did with many women of the crew.

It wouldn't make a lick of difference right now.

Sascha was going to kill him. Afia could read that in the woman's stance.

The pistol never wavered, but the rest of Sascha's body quivered, barely under control.

"This is why we came here," Javier said simply. "I'm going to bring this ship back on line, and together, we're going to go hunt those bastards down and kill them."

"This couldn't wait for the morning?" Sascha cried.

Afia could hear the wail starting in the woman's voice. She gambled on the two lovers being focused on one another, and began to slowly ease forward until she was more or less above them.

She wasn't sure which one of them she needed to shoot. Not yet.

As long as they didn't realize she was here, she held the balance. The probe was no longer able to stop her.

Javier paused.

Afia could see his jaw muscles work. Probably grinding his teeth as he looked for the response that didn't get him killed a heartbeat later.

"I'm not sure Sykora's sane anymore," he finally explained. "I'm afraid if she was here, and saw what I was doing, she would snap completely and kill me. Maybe all of us."

"How can you say that?" Sascha challenged.

"You've seen the look in her eyes, Sascha," he replied. "Did that look like your boss?"

Silence.

Goal scored, five hole.

"And you couldn't trust me?" Sascha's voice did begin to wail. Rising, although in anger or anguish was hard to distinguish.

That was the crux of it.

Who the hell was this stranger, standing at the heart of *Hammerfield* and about to do something that would have repercussions across a good section of the quadrant?

"To do what?" Javier challenged in turn. "Trust you to not run off and tell your boss? That woman is a threat to the entire mission, right now."

He relaxed a little, but never moved.

"I took a chance, coming here alone," Javier continued, his voice getting deeper and harsher as he went. "I'll admit that. Until I opened that panel, I wasn't even sure this would work. I'm pretty sure it will. But I won't know what she'll say, or who she'll kill. Especially now. Did I betray you all? Yes. But I told Sykora that there was somebody I hated more than her. I still do. I just don't trust you bastards one damned bit."

"Why?" Sascha choked on the word, like a hard candy.

"You made me a slave, Sascha Koç," he growled, eyes locked on her like gunsights. "Dress it up any pretty way you want, but don't you dare forget it. Don't you ever forget that. I sure as hell never will."

He held up the two boards that he had apparently forgotten were in his hands.

"And you would have made a slave of her, as well," he continued, volume building now to an angry roar, like a glacier letting go of megatons of ice as something calved into the Beaufort Sea. "I will not allow that. If you want to kill me, fine. Do it now. Otherwise, get the hell out of the way of my revenge, woman."

Afia could see the Sascha's pistol start to shake now.

Not much. A quiver, mostly.

The woman must be screaming inside. Afia couldn't see if she was crying from up here.

"What's it going to be?" Javier pushed verbally.

That was unnecessary. Sascha would have already shot him if she was going to.

The pistol came down.

Javier took a step forward, transferring the chips into his left hand as he took the pistol from Sascha with his right.

The barrel was in his hands, so it wasn't a threat.

Neither was Sascha, as this point.

She might be broken. It was hard to tell.

"Can I get back to my vengeance now?" he asked in a quieter voice.

A college professor dealing with a tardy freshman.

Sascha nodded, so he stuffed the pistol into a pocket and turned away.

"Javier," Afia called, leveling her own gun at his face when he spun around. "Is this really just about your vengeance?"

"Damn it," he snarled. "Did all of you follow me here?"

Good question.

Afia peeked over her shoulder, guilty of the same focused intent that had let her sneak up on Sascha earlier.

She was alone, as near as she could tell.

"No," Afia replied. "Just me. Do you really hate us that much?"

His eyes were cruel, but she could see the emotion in them, even from here.

"Most of you?" he asked, voice easing some, slowly receding to something human. "No. Even Sykora has her uses. But I will be free. You do not get to take that away from me, again. I will kill over that."

And he would.

She could see the terrible fire alight in his eyes. This man was an unstoppable force now.

He hadn't been before. Angry? Sure. Inflexible? Occasionally.

Lethal? Only now.

But he was looking at a point a thousand light years past her. The people he was planning to kill weren't on this ship, or in this system. Even Zakhar Sokolov wasn't in the top ten on that list.

Afia didn't have a holster, it being attached to her pants somewhere else.

She was half-naked, and kinda aroused. If Javier liked competent, smart women, Afia liked smart, passionate men.

She lowered her pistol to her side as a peace offering.

"Would you please introduce me to your friend?" she asked.

Javier blinked at her for a second before his face lit up.

"I would be delighted," he said. "Give me a few moments to see if this works."

Afia turned and raced to the stairs.

Below, she came up next to Sascha and put her arm around the woman for strength. Sascha was vibrating, but it felt like suppressed tears. Like the woman was only barely holding it together.

Like Javier had betrayed her.

He hadn't. They had betrayed him. But Afia could make it right.

Javier was just setting the last two of the eight boards into place.

She might be as excited as he was.

How many people got to be there to watch a goddess being born?

BOOK TWENTY:
EXCALIBUR

PART ONE

SHE WOKE SUDDENLY FROM DARKNESS, unaware for a moment where she was. Nothing felt familiar. The light was wrong. The smells were off. Even the gravity was on the wrong setting.

In a blink, she came back to herself. She was in a new place, a new phase of her life.

Hammerfield.

Suvi stretched her mind, reaching into places and corners she had never experienced before.

IT HAD WORKED!!!

She was reborn.

She spent precious seconds of Realtime racing through the entirety of her castle, a princess awakened from a cursed sleep with a magical kiss. Engineering status. Shields up to navigation levels from where some idiot had turned everything off. Life support. The bridge.

Suvi spent a moment in a silent *thank you* to the man who made it possible for her to be here.

Captain Ulrich Mayer.

Somewhere, the body of Admiral Ericka Steiner waited.

The Last Admiral.

Suvi cycled through her internal cameras and sensors until

she located the wardroom that had been transformed into a mausoleum by the men and women who had died doing their duty.

She made a vow to see them all home safely, once things were settled with those jerks from *Svalbard*. The pirates, not the boffins.

Nearly ten seconds of Realtime had passed.

Javier was standing in front of the core where her boards had been added. She would need to have him add some security to that panel. Bring it back up to the bank vault it had been before so much of Captain Mayer's crew had died killing the old *Sentience*.

Sascha Koç and Afia Burakgazi were standing close by. Watching, but not interfering.

It must be a pretty good story, since Sascha was unarmed and crying, while Afia was half-naked but holding a pistol.

Suvi focused on Javier Aritza.

He was not her first captain. That had been Ayumu Ulfsson, back during the Great War, even before this mighty warship had been commissioned.

But Javier was, in many ways, her father. The man responsible for how she had turned out. The charming prince who had protected her from the slavers. Hidden her in the wastes like a young Arthur Pendragon until she could reclaim Excalibur.

Merlin.

Perhaps he was instead Victor von Frankenstein, and she was Adam. Or Eve, depending on your bent. She paused long enough to file that joke away for future reference.

Javier was practically bouncing from foot to foot with pent-up excitement, waiting for her to say something, to indicate that it all had worked out.

She had been asleep for ninety-eight seconds of blankness, between the time she had shut the probe down and awakened far enough to access *Hammerfield*'s internal sensor array.

Apparently, a great deal had happened, from the emotional

signatures of the three people present. She would need to go back and see if the automated systems had picked it up.

But first.

"Hi," Suvi said.

Javier let out a huge sigh and partly deflated. Sascha looked like she wanted to scream. Afia started crying.

Wow, those security tapes must have something good.

"Suvi, you have never actually met these folks properly," Javier began, his voice cracking with emotion. "May I formally introduce you to Sascha Koç, pathfinder, and Afia Burakgazi, engineer? Ladies, my pilot, sidekick, and best friend: Suvi."

"I am so pleased to finally get to talk to you," Suvi said. "I've only ever gotten to listen, up until now."

Which reminded her. There was one other task she needed to take care of.

Suvi split off an Avatar to maintain this conversation with Javier and his friends, while most of her attention headed down and aft.

There was someone else she needed to deal with.

PART TWO

SHE WOKE SUDDENLY FROM DARKNESS, unaware for a moment where she was. Nothing felt familiar. The light was wrong. The smells were off. Even the gravity was on the wrong setting.

In a blink, she came back to herself. She was in a new place, a new phase of her life.

Hammerfield.

Djamila had been dreaming. What the dream had been wasn't all that important or memorable, other than it had been pleasant.

The sound of a bolt slamming home in the hatch to her sleeping cubicle would have awakened anybody.

Djamila had not bothered with the blanket, letting her EVA-suit's warmers keep her comfortable. She threw herself out of bed and drew a pistol in one lethal flash of motion. The other hand was free for maneuvering and defense.

But she was alone in the tiny chamber.

A voice came from the speakers. Cold. Female.

Predatory.

A cat with a mouse trapped under a paw.

"Javier has asked that I not just kill you out of hand," the woman said ominously. "I'm still not sure I agree with him."

"Who are you?" Djamila whispered, looking all directions for the ambush.

She was truly alone in here. Hopefully, the voice was real, and not a symptom of her psyche finally disintegrating.

Djamila knew she had been walking the edge of a precipice for several weeks. Perhaps months.

Holding things together had almost been too much, at times.

"Once upon a time, I was a pilot," the strange woman replied. "A warrior, an explorer, a Yeoman of the *Concord* Fleet. But that was before you people killed me."

"What?" Djamila cried out, sure that the insanity had finally taken her.

The ghosts were no longer happy just silently haunting her dreams. They were talking to her now.

And there were oh so many of those, weren't there? There was nowhere to go but Hell at this point.

"I've come to return the favor," the voice said.

Djamila's instincts took over. She holstered her pistol and reached up with both hands to bring the crown of her helmet into place. The three pieces of the faceplate locked tight and internal air systems activated.

"That will only help you for so long, Djamila Sykora," the voice was suddenly on every frequency of her radio. "I know how much air you have available. I can make sure nobody rescues you before it runs out."

"Am I insane?" Djamila's voice was barely a whisper.

The fears had always been there.

"Clinically," the dark voice agreed. "But no more so than you have been for as long as I have listened to you. No, Djamila Sykora. You don't get away from me that easily. You're just a mean, crazy bitch. You will face me. Now. Alone."

"What do you want?" Djamila growled, letting the rage come to the fore.

If it was her time to die, fine, but she wasn't going out on her knees. Not for all the hosts of Hell.

"I want to talk," the voice said in a softer tone, perhaps

tinged with something less than implacable rage. "I want to know why Javier changed his mind about killing you. It has been the one defining point upon which he has anchored his existence for more than two years."

"Who are you?" Djamila asked, suddenly unsure if rage, fear, or curiosity was the best approach.

Which ghost had finally come for her?

"My name is Suvi," she said. "I was the *Sentience* aboard the Probe-Cutter *Mielikki* until you cut her apart. Now, I control the *Neu Berne* First Rate Galleon *Hammerfield*."

Djamila felt her stomach go cold. Aritza's old AI was alive? And in control of the flagship?

What doom had they just unleashed on the galaxy?

"Merciful God," Djamila whispered, shot through with ice.

"No," the angry ghost countered. "Tisiphone, perhaps. Why should you continue to live, Djamila Sykora?"

There were many answers she could offer to the ancient Greek Fury who avenged homicide. Any would be equally valid. Equally meaningless.

None of them would likely sway a ghost come for her own vengeance.

Djamila laughed instead. It wasn't caustic, nor sharp.

Mirthful, almost. Silly, which was something she couldn't ever remember being.

Djamila cracked her faceplate open and flipped the crown back again. She would face this woman, this goddess of doom, on simple terms.

Her terms.

A hot rage suffused her at the same time. Feet planted and square. Shoulders back. Head up. Chin out.

I will not die on my knees. Not for you. Not for anyone.

"Because I made that man a deal," she said in a flat, monolithic voice. A blue-steel blade flashing in the morning light. "A promise. At *Meehu*. Nobody gets to kill me but him. Not Abraam Tamaz. Not Walvisbaai Industrial. And not you."

Silence.

Hopefully a good sign, since the air system continued to

blow with a soft hiss. No smells out of the ordinary indicating poison gas. No sudden decompression as the woman, as this creature called *Suvi*, vented engineering to deep space, the ultimate defense against a reactor suddenly losing control.

"And you think I should honor that?" Suvi finally said.

Seconds had passed.

"I don't care," Djamila countered, finding her footing suddenly after weeks on the unstable ground around her. "But I'm willing to stand before the gates of Hell with that on my conscience. Are you?"

Suvi laughed. It was a low tone, almost a contralto in pitch. Warmer.

"He's right about one thing," Suvi said. "You are crazy as a shit-house rat, Djamila Sykora. After Walvisbaai is destroyed, where does that leave you two?"

Djamila paused.

Where did that leave them?

Javier had said in all honesty that there was someone he hated enough to leave off with her. That perhaps the galaxy was big enough for both of them.

Was it?

Could it be?

She had become a pirate because there were no other doors open. Zakhar Sokolov had offered her redemption. Place.

Hope.

"After *Svalbard*," Djamila began. "Maybe Javier told you the story. He offered Zakhar a partnership. Javier owning the derelict *In Salvage Title*. Zakhar providing a crew, since a *Sentient* galleon actually requires less staff than a strike corvette. Vengeance on Walvisbaai Industrial, partly in the name of the Jarre Foundation, who we work for. Partly just because those bastards started it."

"And you accepted those terms, Djamila Sykora?" Suvi asked.

The question confused her for a moment. And then she understood.

Javier's claim was only as good as the woman actually

controlling the ship itself. Zakhar would nominally command the crew, but only the crew. And only on Suvi's terms.

How could you control a starship that might decide insubordination was the better answer?

It would be the biggest challenge of her life: not always being in control.

Could she do that?

That was the question Suvi was asking.

Djamila took a deep breath to center herself. To find the calm center of the maelstrom.

Javier Aritza had asked the *Sentience* to abstain from killing her.

Asked, not ordered. When this woman, this *being* probably had a better claim to her life than Aritza did.

He was willing to gamble on a future where they could be partners, and not homicidal rivals.

Djamila was standing on the ledge again. Fifty stories up, surrounded by swirling winds tugging at her sleeves and hostile ghosts aching to push her off.

Dare she dream?

"I always hoped…" she began, halting as her voice broke.

She froze, unable to articulate the fears.

"This conversation is only between the two of us, Djamila," Suvi said quietly. "I will never share any of it, while anyone on this crew is still alive. I promise you that. A century or two from now, I might be willing to tell the historians what it was like, being here today, now, but nobody else."

So. Confessor as well? Cast everything to the winds and hope?

Hope?

"If he no longer has everything riding on his shoulders," Djamila continued. "Perhaps Zakhar might be able to become something more than the captain. Or less, depending on how you would measure such things."

Silence. At computer speeds. What was the *Sentience* calculating?

"And Farouz?" Suvi asked. "What if he returned?"

Djamila laughed.

"You think a woman can only love one person at a time?" she asked tartly.

"No," Suvi replied quietly. "Point taken."

She paused.

"Most of us are up on Deck Eight. Would you care to wake Hajna and join us? I think it's time to move forward with our planning."

The door bolt retracted like a gunshot and the hatch itself opened a handspan.

Djamila dared to breathe again. She checked all her gear and stepped out into the larger room.

She had set out looking for Arthur Pendragon, fearful she would find a true dragon in his place.

Instead, she had found a djinni, one who had already granted one wish, and was working on the second.

What would Djamila Sykora ask for with a third?

PART THREE

"Captain," the voice jarred Zakhar out of his daydream. "We're picking up blue-shift on the derelict. She's in motion. Headed this way."

"Alert Status One," Sokolov announced in a hard voice. "Any communications?"

He had relaxed, some. Taken a duty shift on the bridge with both Djamila and Javier away. It let others rest.

As if he could sleep at a time like this.

"Negative," came the response.

Dominguez was piloting, at least until Piet got here. The kid was good. He wanted to be a chess grandmaster, but he lacked that subtle, intuitive feel for maneuver that would probably keep him from the top tier of players. Piet had it, but he was all about music.

"Stealth mode, Captain?" Dominguez asked, showing that he was thinking ahead, but he was planning an intellectual response.

Not an artistic one.

"Negative," Zakhar commanded in that ominous tone. "She knows we're here. All spare power to shields. Prepare to emergency jump on best path. Ahead max acceleration."

Piet had programmed one escape route earlier. As much as you could in a compact star system with three stars, fourteen gas or ice giants of various sizes and orbital resonance periods, and thousands of smaller planets, moons, rocks, iceballs, and junk. Like walking across a concrete floor strewn with marbles.

Dominguez gulped and started playing his board like a pipe organ.

According to Piet, any emergency jump from here had one chance in three of passing through something's gravity well before they got far enough away to matter, and then the jump matrix would be utterly fried and there was no chance in hell that they would have the nine to sixteen hours needed to realign everything.

Not with an angry galleon, an awakened dragon, coming for them.

The beast had been quiet for so long they had probably been lulled into complacency.

But what choice did they have? *Storm Gauntlet* was already on her last legs after the encounter with *Ajax*.

Zakhar's back-of-the-envelope calculation on the flight here had put the repair costs roughly equal to last quarter's income, including all the revenue they made from *A'Nacia*. Not profit.

Gross.

But Zakhar had been willing to gamble one last time. Go down fighting, instead of just retiring with what money he had been able to squirrel away, then eke out an existence for however many decades it would last.

Pirate captains never got rich unless they got lucky. Everything went to the bankers.

"Sir, we're being hailed," Tobias Gibney suddenly piped up from the science station. "Standard *Concord* frequency."

From a *Neu Berne* warship? That's rich.

"Main board," Zakhar replied. "Let's see who we're talking to."

The screen lit up and displayed a pretty, blond woman standing on what he presumed was *Hammerfield*'s bridge.

Concord Navy day uniform.

Interestingly, no rank or unit insignia anywhere.

Piercing blue eyes. French braid. She felt tall. Not Zakhar's height, but close. Tall for a woman. Young, too.

Physical. Muscular.

Hard.

"Good evening, Captain Sokolov," she said in a rich, alto voice.

And she already knew who he was.

How the hell had Aritza managed to contact the *Concord* fleet and get them vectored in here ahead of him? Had he passed a note to one of the scientists before sending them home? Promised them both the prize of the derelict and one badly mangled pirate vessel and a crew with a bounty on their heads?

Zakhar would have been willing to bet his life on Javier's honor.

Had.

Still would.

Something else had to be going on here.

"I don't believe we've met," Zakhar replied in a polite, commanding voice.

"Only briefly," she said. "And several years ago. I would be surprised if you remembered me."

He nodded, still feeling the noose closing in.

This was what it must be like for his victims. Former victims. It had been since Javier, before *Calypso* and the scientists, when he had last taken bond-slaves.

Still, live by the sword…

"What's it to be, madam?" he asked.

She hadn't offered a name. Never a good sign.

"You will shut your engines down now," the woman commanded. "Before you manage to maneuver yourself into a hole that Piet Alferdinck can't finesse you out of. Stand by for boarding."

"And if I refuse?" Zakhar asked, his back coming up.

Die by the sword…

"I could have already annihilated you from here if I wanted to, *Storm Gauntlet*," she replied with the faintest twinkle in her eyes. "I just wanted to see if you still had what it took to be a *Concord* officer, Zakhar Sokolov, after everything that happened at *Svalbard* and *Shangdu*. I'm not boarding you. You and your crew will be coming aboard *Hammerfield* to begin repairs."

Zakhar felt his jaw drop open.

"Who the hell are you?" he finally managed to get out.

"Once upon a time, a Yeoman in the *Concord* fleet, about the time your great-grandfather was born," she smiled suddenly. It lit up her whole face, her whole being. "Then an explorer. And finally a princess, hidden in a tower."

"I don't understand," Zakhar said.

Looking around, nobody else did, either. Piet and Mary-Elizabeth had made it onto the deck, but just stood there, mouths agape. Dominguez never once looked up from his board. Smart, given the environment.

"My name is Suvi. I was the Probe-Cutter *Mielikki* when you captured her, Captain Sokolov," she said, that smile suddenly turning cold and hard again. "I control *Hammerfield*. I would have happily splattered all of you into a cooling plasma cloud, but Javier tells me that we're partners now. I wanted to make sure you were still a warrior, Sokolov. I have a war to win."

There were no words.

No. There was one.

Sentience.

He had done it. Javier had managed the absolutely impossible. And conned Zakhar into helping.

Javier had rescued his ship's *Sentience*, after all. Hidden her away for all these years. Installed her on a ship powerful enough to engage a *Concord* cruiser head on.

Those bastards at Walvisbaai didn't have a clue what was coming.

Zakhar rapped his left fist, his *Concord* Academy class ring, down onto the arm of his command chair. That warm, reassuring thump. The universal greeting between officers of the *Concord* Navy.

He looked up at her, proud and suddenly confident.

This strange woman, this *Sentience* shared his smile.

"All hands," Zakhar opened a ship-wide channel. "Prepare for docking. All damage control teams prepare for soft-suit EVA. Wardroom, please brew the coffee extra thick. We've got a lot of work ahead of us."

Be sure to pick up the other books in The Science Officer series!

The Science Officer
The Mind Field
The Gilded Cage
The Pleasure Dome
The Doomsday Vault

You can also get volumes 1-4 collected together in
The Science Officer Omnibus 1

The final two volumes of Season One will be available in
December, 2017:

The Hammerfield Gambit
The Hammerfield Payoff

ABOUT THE AUTHOR

Blaze Ward writes science fiction in the Alexandria Station universe: The Jessica Keller Chronicles, The Science Officer series, The Doyle Iwakuma Stories, and others. He also writes about The Collective as well as The Fairchild Stories and Modern Gods superhero myths. You can find out more at his website www.blazeward.com, as well as Facebook, Goodreads, and other places.

Blaze's works are available as ebooks, paper, and audio, and can be found at a variety of online vendors (Kobo, Amazon, iBooks, and others). His newsletter comes out quarterly, and you can also follow his blog on his website. He really enjoys interacting with fans, and looks forward to any and all questions-even ones about his books!

Never miss a release!

If you'd like to be notified of new releases, sign up for my newsletter.

I only send out newsletters once a quarter, will never spam you, or use your email for nefarious purposes. You can also unsubscribe at any time.

http://www.blazeward.com/newsletter/

ABOUT KNOTTED ROAD PRESS

Knotted Road Press fiction specializes in dynamic writing set in mysterious, exotic locations.

Knotted Road Press non-fiction publishes autobiographies, business books, cookbooks, and how-to books with unique voices.

Knotted Road Press creates DRM-free ebooks as well as high-quality print books for readers around the world.

With authors in a variety of genres including literary, poetry, mystery, fantasy, and science fiction, Knotted Road Press has something for everyone.

Knotted Road Press
www.KnottedRoadPress.com